Rachel H. Kester

AMISH CROSSROADS SERIES

Box Set: Book 1-4

Amish Crossroads Series

A note for our readers...

You are going to read 4 episodes of the series Amish Crossroads.

If you enjoy these books, make sure to sign up here:

http://www.amishromanceseries.com/amish-crossroad/

for information about next releases, discount offers and FREE book from Rachel H. Kester and other great Amish Romance Series authors.

It's completely free, and never miss all the best in the incredible world of the Amish Romance Series.

Lastly, you will find in this book some uncommon words in italics, they are not English, but Amish. We will send to you a list with the translation of all the main Amish words as soon as you will be register to:

http://www.amishromanceseries.com/amish-crossroad/

We look forward to reading with you ;-)
Sincerely Yours.

Table of Contents

Rachel H. Kester

Amish Crossroads Series

BOOK 1 – Family Obstacles

Rachel H. Kester

Chapter 1

As I sit here milking the cow, I realize that I really didn't do a very good job of warming up my hands for Betsy. I would have jumped just as high as she did if I had somebody touching me like that. I should have been more careful, but my mind has been preoccupied with other things lately. I lost my husband two years ago and it still hurts to this day. You'd think that I might be bitter that he left me alone like this, but I can take solace in knowing that *Gott* needed him back by his side. The doctors say it was an aneurysm, but I don't believe in such nonsense. It was *Gott*'s way of saying that it was his time and there was nothing that I or anybody else was going to do about that.

"Mommy, can I do that?" Rebekah, my *bobli*, well she's not exactly a baby anymore and I shouldn't be treating her as such. She is such a little lady, sitting beside me while I milk the cow and wanting more than anything to help me out. She has always been a precocious child, someone that needed to get her hands into just about everything. I was kind of proud to see how much she had grown up over these last two years.

Her blonde hair is the perfect length, tied into a ponytail and lifted above her shoulders with a pin to keep it in place. Her white bonnet is exactly like the one I had. I guess I really do have a knack for this type of work. I've also learned how to feed the chickens and basically do whatever my husband Holden used to do when he was around. My mother in law Henrietta has come to live with me to help out, but her health is failing and she has trouble breathing when it's cold outside. She has taken over my chores with preparing breakfast. I will say that having Uncle James around has helped a lot, but for the most part we were alone.

"I wouldn't in such a hurry to grow up if I were you, because you're only a child once. I want you to remain as innocent as possible," I said while I patted Rebekah on the shoulder.

"Mommy, when is daddy back from his trip?" I didn't have the heart to tell her when she was only three years old that her father was never coming back. I told her that he was on an extended trip and left it at that. I knew that I was going to have to have this conversation with her, but I wasn't sure she would understand the aspect of death. I might have to get Bishop Alba to help me with this matter. He has always been there for me since my husband's untimely demise. I did take Rebekah to the funeral, but she was too young to understand.

"Not for a little while, but I'm sure that he's thinking about you all the time." This gave her a moment of complete childlike bliss as her smile was etched across her face. She began to skip around with her bare feet touching the sodden grass. She was enjoying the feeling of freedom that came from being so young.

My mother in law come out the patio door with it swinging behind her. "Bethany, I thought that I would come out and lend a hand, but I see that you have everything well in hand. Breakfast is almost ready, and all we need is the eggs to complete the meal."

"I'm just about done, Henrietta."

I had already gotten the eggs from the chickens, which were already in a basket beside me ready to take inside. Henrietta kneeled down and said. "By the way, I was talking to our neighbor Julie and she has informed me that you're thinking about becoming a volunteer aid worker. I don't know if that's a good idea. I think that your *dochtah* and I need you more than anybody else." I should've known that Julie would be gossiping. I wouldn't be surprised if the whole district knew what I was thinking.

"I haven't decided anything yet and I'm just mulling over my options." It was the best way to appease her, because she was always telling me that I needed to keep family as close as possible. With my Amish upbringing, I learned that family was the most important thing and that we always took care of one another before going outside of the home. It was just that I had too many memories. I looked around at every aspect of this house and I saw my husband staring back at me all the time. "I won't do anything until I talk to you about it and I promise that I'll make sure that both of you are taken care of, even if I am away for a short period of time."

"I don't like it, Bethany and I don't think my son would approve." She grabbed for the basket, taking it out of my hands and stomping off mumbling underneath her breath. There had always been this wall between us, but I think she softened after Holden died. It took a toll on her physically, but I couldn't have asked for a better mother in law to take care of Rebekah. She was always doting on her, playing with her and making her feel special. What more could a child ask for.

Unfortunately, I have lost out on a lot of her growing up, because my time was now devoted to making sure that we were all fed, clothed and had a roof over our heads. I did this by selling my sewing at the market and at small local stores outside of the Amish community. I was quite amazed that people had taken a shine to my work, so much so that they really couldn't keep them on the shelf. Mostly, I made blankets and scarves, which were homemade and crafted with my own hands.

"Rebekah, I think that your grandmother would like some help with breakfast. Why don't you go in and make sure that the table is set and I'll be right in." Rebekah turned, gave me this pouty little smile. She bounded off with her two little legs moving at a speed that I used to have when I was in my youth.

It feels like a lifetime since he's been gone and I still feel like a piece of me has gone with him. I don't know how to convey that to Henrietta, but I think deep down she probably feels the same thing as a mother. I guess we bonded after his loss, but now I was beginning to think that there had to be more, I knew that we were going to butt heads once again. I decided to take a walk and clear my head.

Chapter 2

"I don't get it, Jacob. You are 19 years old, a good honest man with a work ethic that makes mine pale in comparison. Why you don't have a wife or at least a girl that you're interested in is beyond me. Now you tell me that you want to take your expertise as a carpenter and help those in need. How am I supposed to take it, that you want to leave the family behind? It's not normal. Your place is with this district and by the side of your family."

I had stopped to catch my bonnet. I didn't mean to overhear a conversation, but they were loud.

"I think the rumspringa made me see that there were more things in heaven and earth than just what I see around here. *Gott* has always been my example. Did you know that Jesus himself used to go out to the masses to clean their feet and worship among them?"

"Jacob, I don't need you to quote scripture to me. I go to church every Sunday and I know all about what *Gott* did for us. Now, I think you owe your *maemm* an apology. She has been crying over the possibility of your leaving. I want you to march into that *haus* and tell her that you've changed your mind. I never want to see a tear from her because of you."

"I'll do it, but it's going to be under duress and not at all from the heart."

"Wunderbarr, just as long as you do it." His father Jeremy was standing there with *kaffe*, drinking it like he always did, completely black and without sugar or cream. I will admit that once you have a cup of his *kaffe*, you could work long hours of the day. It was the kind of caffeine fix that gave you the stamina to complete a day's hard labor. He always brought enough for everybody at the church every Sunday.

The young man was cutting wood and had his sleeves rolled up. He was slamming that axe so hard into the logs that they were splitting on the first strike.

"Father, I hope you know that it was you that gave me the courage to take this step. The way that you came to the rescue and helped build that barn last week made me see that I could do the same thing but in an entirely different way."

I saw him run his hand through his *brau* hair and saw the sweat dripping down onto his shaven face.

Just watching him over the years, I saw that he was a true man with a hard exterior from being raised with strict discipline. I've never talked to him, but now I see we might be on the same road in life.

"Jacob, I've never raised a son that would leave his family. I think that you should talk to the Bishop before you make any rash decisions." He had his straw hat on top of his head, and they both had their hands casually placed in between their suspenders as they talked. I saw Jeremy doing that at church and when he was spouting one of his Sermons to Jacob and his *maemm*. I'd heard that his father allowed him to pick up the slack when he got injured on the job. He's still stubborn and doesn't sit still, but I can see that Jacob does what he can to do most of the work.

I watch as he pulls those horses into the field, walking behind them as they plowed with the greatest of ease. It's hard work and I see Jacob look at himself in the reflection of the glass of the kitchen window. I wonder what he's thinking.

I watched from behind a tree, as he finished up this work and then went in and talked to his *maemm*. I think I heard over the wind as he told her that no decisions had been made and that he was really just talking out of turn.

I could already smell the fresh loaf of bread that his mother was cooking in the wood stove. The one thing that I knew from a very early age was that my mother had culinary skills that went beyond just the norm. I think that was one of the reasons why my father married her in the first place. One taste of her shoofly pie and any man in their right mind would fall head over heels.

I was on my way into town to talk to the Bishop. He really was a wise counsel and had a lot to say on the subject of family. When he spoke in church, everybody listened because he had this booming voice that carried like the waves crashing against the shore. Living in Wisconsin, I really didn't have any real knowledge of being on a beach, but I've seen photos to make me yearn to see it myself.

Chapter 3

I had never been one for bundling. I've known a couple of young women that have gone down that road and regretted it. Of course, if they repented and asked for *Gott* 's forgiveness, they would be given a second chance. But that would never take away from the evil stares that they had to contend with every day. Even now, Greta was a bit of a pariah, but nobody said anything to her and mostly it was behind her back.

I was quite happy to see that she was here at the meeting. Around the table there were the perfect complement of six women and six guys sitting around and talking about what it would be like to take on humanitarian aid work.

I can hear every word that the bishop is saying, but my eyes narrow on Jacob. His crooked smile and the way that his dimples crease across his face gives him a boyish look that makes me feel like I am too old for anybody like him. I was only 25, but I had grown up to be more of an adult in the last two years than I've ever known before.

Bishop Alba stood at the head of the table "This is not quite the turnout that I was expecting, but I appreciate everybody coming. I know that you've all been thinking about joining the cause. I have to give you credit for making this leap of faith. It can't be easy on you or your *shtamm*. I've already told you that I would be honored if you would allow me to speak to your loved ones on your behalf. I've already done it for several of you, but I've not had the pleasure of Jacob's or Bethany's *shtamm*." As my name was mentioned, I turn my head, but not before I saw that Jacob was also looking at me from across the table. "I think that the both of you should talk. You're both in the same predicament. I think that both of you can give some sage advice to each other."

As everybody else filed out, I saw that Jacob was the man that I had been looking at. I've only seen him from time to time in town with his father, but every time there always seemed to be some kind of argument going on between them. I've known the Millers for some time, but our families have never really been able to sit down and be in the same room together. The only place that we were ever at that I would see them was at church. It was obvious from a very early age that they didn't really like each other. I had no idea why, but I sensed that it had to be quite personal and none of my business.

Jacob stammered "This whole thing has been quite daunting. I don't suppose you have any advice for a *mann* that can't get his family to listen to reason." I almost burst out laughing, because I could almost feel that we were kindred spirits. "I don't see anything amusing about any of this."

I didn't know that I was smiling. I certainly didn't want him to think that I was making fun of what he was going through "I'm smiling because I'm going through the same thing with my mother in law and having a *dochtah* still very young is making this even harder." We both had the bible, the King James version in front of us. I could sense that he got the same comfort from its pages as I did.

"I'm sorry for being so defensive, but we both know that we live a life of submission and simplicity," Jacob said. "Don't get me wrong, I enjoy my life, but I really want to help those that can't help themselves. I don't know why that is so wrong."

Jacob was only saying the same thing that I was thinking. It was in his eyes that I saw the conviction of a man that wanted to do the right thing for everybody concerned. It was the first time that we had ever talked openly and honestly to each other. For the most part our families were split down the middle.

It was the first time that I saw that he was a strapping young man, but it was his family commitment that made him more attractive. It didn't hurt that he had the bluest eyes and a smile that lit up the room. I could even see the bulging muscles underneath his white shirt. I could almost envision him in the yard working with his sleeves rolled up.

It was interesting to be in this church, especially since it was not really a church to begin with. We were in this old barn that had stood up to the test of time over the years. It was just a place to meet and talk. Every family took on the commitment of taking on Sunday Services in their house once a year. If the house wasn't big enough, it would be held in the barn.

"Jacob, I don't know why they just don't understand that we want to help. I know that family comes first, but we've learned that obedience was the most important thing and the rest would follow. We follow the *Ordnung* to the letter. I don't know how to make my mother in law see that I need this time to find myself."

His eyes were now showing compassion, which came from the knowledge that I had just lost my husband two years ago. I never thought that I would find another, but now I was beginning to see that maybe there was room in my heart for somebody else.

"I really enjoyed our conversation, Bethany and I would like to continue to talk. I don't want to be presumptuous, but I was hoping that you would want to do the same thing." All I could do was nod my head, because he really did take me by surprise by what he said. "I'm glad to hear that. I don't know when I've ever had a stress free day in my life."

We made plans to meet up, but we would have to do it so that the two families wouldn't find out about it. We already had enough problems getting them to relinquish hold, so that we could go do some aid work, which meant that we really didn't need the added headache of the animosity between them.

Chapter 4

It had been two weeks and it was some the best moments of my life. We talked and actually got to know each other. I found him to be open and honest, willing to compromise and even finding that he was a caring man. The way that he talked about his mother made me know just what kind of man he was. He never said a bad word about her. Yet underneath everything that he was saying, I could sense that he was hitting a brick wall with the both of them.

"I don't know how you thought you were going to hide this from us, but Henrietta was very forthcoming in telling us what you've been up to. The Millers are not our kind of people. We've told you that from the moment that you were old enough to understand." My own mother Susan was now grilling me, telling me who I could see and who I couldn't. Making a point by bringing my father Christian into it as well.

He was more quiet and standoffish, smoking his pipe and sitting there and listening to everything that was being said.

My father said "I don't say much, but what I do know is that your *maemm* is right." Of course he would take her side in this, because he really didn't want to find himself in the dog house. I'd gotten my stubbornness from my mother. Putting us in the same room together was just going to make things strained between us. "Just listen to your *maemm* and do what she tells you to do." My Father Christian was always a good provider, but he never really wanted to get into the middle of it, between my *maemm* and I. For the most part, he would hear any argument that we were having and then go out to the barn to work.

He was never into conflict, but if we couldn't work it out together, then he would step in and put his foot down. "It's not like I'm going to marry him. I'm just spending time with him to figure out what I'm going to do."

She turned abruptly, grabbed me by the shoulders and then looked me in the eye. "That's another thing that we don't condone. Your place is with your *dochtah* and Henrietta. Have you thought about what's going to happen to them if you take off on this insane quest for finding yourself?"

"I haven't thought of anything else and I'm putting things into place that would make their life easier." I heard the knocking on the door. I wasn't quite sure how I knew it, but I sensed into my very bones that Jacob was on the other side. I had told him everything that was going on with my family. He turned to me and told me that things didn't have to be so hard.

I had just about had it with anybody trying to tell me what to do and I sighed with a sort of defeated attitude, before turning my back on my mother and father. I then walked out that door to face Jacob. "I don't think you really want to go in there. If I were you, I think that you should come with me and get away from here as soon as possible." I could see that he was about to say something, but I put my finger on to his lips to quiet any sort of argument. "Believe me, this is the last place you want to be, Jacob."

We walked away with me glancing over my shoulder to see that my mother and father were now staring at us both from the window. It was a wonder that they didn't come out and grab me by the hair and pull me back into the house. I was glad that they didn't.

"Bethany, I heard some of the things that were being said. I guess I thought that I should come to the rescue." He had his hands in between his suspenders, like he was an orator at some kind of trial. I've noticed that about him, but I would never try to change him for something that he wasn't. "I want you to know that whatever you decide is perfectly fine with me. I've been hitting a few road blocks myself. My *daed* has been hinting that he is not as young as he used to be. Just between you and me, I believe that my *maemm* has been whispering things into his ears. I don't think he's all that fragile. I've seen him at *schaffe* to know that the pain is manageable."

"Jacob, I know how much your family means to you and I would never tell you to walk away from them. This has to be your decision, but I will listen to everything you have to say." The only thing we really needed to know was that we were getting closer. He had just started to hold my hand in a very discreet and romantic way. His fingers were entwined around my own and I would feel this flutter in my chest. It felt like I was alive, breathing a breath of air that felt too good to be true.

"Bethany, I really never thought that they would be so against me helping others. They have read the same Bible that I have and they know that helping others is part of the reason why *Gott* came down here in the first place. I don't know what to do. I'm at my wits end. It's the same thing every day. I'm getting tired of having the same conversation over and over again. They won't listen and I know they love me, but they certainly don't show it in the way that I would want them to." His hand had now touched the back of mine. I really don't think he knew what he was doing.

"Jacob, I do believe that everything will work out. Eventually both of our family's will see that this is best for you and me." I wasn't sure who I was trying to convince, him or me. But thankfully I got a meek mile in return for my wisdom on the subject.

"From your lips to *Gott* 's ears." He leaned in and moved the hair away from my ears, sending a shiver down my spine, but not taking it any further than that.

I'd already been courted by my husband. I then went through the *Zeugnis* with the bishop, before marrying in front of all my friends and family. It was a wonderful day, sunny and magical. It was everything that I would have hoped for and more. It felt like I was going against his memory by being with Jacob, but I couldn't help the way that he made me feel.

Chapter 5

Over the next couple of days, I started to know that Jacob was feeling the same thing for me as I was feeling for him. It was the way that he looked me, held my hand and touched me innocently. It wasn't just that he was gorgeous, but in the Biblical sense, he was exactly my type on the inside and the outside. His beliefs were more my own. We also had the same penchant for helping people that was getting us into hot water.

"Bethany, I think that I am falling for you. I don't really know what love is. The only thing I do know is that I miss you when you are gone and I think about you every single minute. I have this yearning to see you. Sometimes it takes all of my effort not to just go running over to your place and knock on your door. This is all so very different for me. I never thought that I would find anybody, especially not a widow that was still getting over the loss of her husband."

"Jacob, you have no idea what your words mean to me. I was thinking that I was in this alone, but it makes my heart sing to know that you feel the same way about me that I feel about you. I've never been one to shy away from my feelings. I guess I have my dear departed husband to thank for that. I was a bit of an introvert. I didn't know quite what to say, but that didn't stop him from coming over to me and talking to me. I always thought that it had taken a lot of courage on his part. I decided from the moment that I met him that I would never walk away from something that meant so much to me." We were sitting underneath this tree, reading from the Bible and praying to God that he would give us guidance to find our way.

He actually brought a couple of cups of *kaffe*, but it was a little strong for my liking. If I didn't know any better, I would think that it was strong enough to grow hair where there was none. He smiled when I made this face, scrunching my features and trying my best not to say anything to go against his father's *kaffe*.

"Bethany, I know all about it, but once you get used to it, it's not so bad." He turned to me and I felt this instant chemistry. Then suddenly his lips were so close to mine that I could almost taste them. We were both hesitant to go any further, but suddenly it was like we both understood what was going to happen before it did. We both moved a little closer at the same time. Our lips touched for that brief second before we pulled away. His face had turned a crimson red. I imagine that he wasn't the only one.

He got up and looked like he had done something wrong. "What am I doing? You're still getting over the loss of your husband. Here I am making it a lot harder on you. I hope you can forgive how forward I was. I didn't mean to make you feel uncomfortable or make you do something that you didn't want to do. I know that it was wrong, but I wouldn't take that kiss back for anything in this world." This was eating him up inside. I didn't want him to feel that he was making me do anything that I didn't want to do.

Getting up on to my feet, I folded down my skirt demurely, while making sure that my legs were covered all the way to the ankles "You don't have to worry about that, Jacob. I wouldn't have allowed you to kiss me if I didn't want to. Yes, I still have a special spot for my husband in my heart, but I also have you to replace that piece that was lost. I don't know how quite to say this, but you really do complete me." I had my hand on his shoulder, seeing his head bowed and then it came back up. He then turned with this brilliant white smile.

"Bethany, there has to be a way for us to be together. They can't keep us apart no matter how much they want to." I wasn't quite sure that we could be together without their blessing. They meant too much for us to walk away from them for the chance at a happiness that we both deserved. We could deny our feelings, but every time we saw each other it would be like a cold slap to the face.

My dark blue skirt was covered with fallen leaves and I had to take a moment to wipe them off, . He touched my hair and pulled the grass clippings that had gotten caught while we were lying down together. "Jacob, everything about you makes me want to know you. Everything I learn about you makes me want to learn more. I've only known one other *mann* that made me feel this way." We had both been spending a lot of time together, knowing full well that our parents and Henrietta didn't approve. We were still doing it nonetheless.

Why Henrietta was getting into the middle of these squabbles is beyond me. If I were to make an educated guess, I would say that she was just jumping on the bandwagon and hoping that I wouldn't leave.

"I think I might have a way to speed things along. I do have to get home because *maemm* is making scrapple and Whoopi pie for dessert." I'd never tried making scrapple, but I've always wanted to give it a go. My claim to fame was my world famous chow chow and I've even canned my own and brought it to the market. Most of my income came from blankets and scarves that I sold in town at a local boutique. They'd taken my designs and before I knew what was happening I had three such stores carrying my stuff. They told me that they had never seen anything so beautiful in their life.

"Jacob, I have some orders to fulfill and my sewing machine has been calling to me the last couple of days. I'm sure that we'll be able to find some common ground. Maybe this rift between them is just something petty and can be fixed over a nice cup of your father's *kaffe*."

"I think that you're giving my father's *kaffe* a lot more credit than it deserves." We both began laughing, so hard and so loud that we almost fell down on to our knees crying at the same time. When we finally got it together, he went through the woods back to his house, while I made my way down the hill and back to the farm that was causing me so much sleepless nights.

Chapter 6

"Jacob, I know that we've been seeing each other for the last couple of weeks, but I need to tell you something. I do hope that you don't take it personally." I had been constantly having one argument after the other with Henrietta and my parents. I didn't know where to turn. I felt like it was time to just give in and do what they wanted me to do. "I know that we promised each other that we would be going together on this humanitarian aid program, but I'm beginning to feel that my place is here." I wanted more than anything to leave with him. This was not a decision that I had made lightly.

He took my hand and I glanced up at him to see that he was about to say something "Bethany, I don't know why we let our family's dictate our lives, but I understand where you're coming from. We both have commitments to our loved ones that makes it harder for us to leave them. I'm also feeling the same conflict. My *maemm* doesn't even talk to me anymore, scoffs when I say anything and just turns her back on me. My father has just about had enough and knows that what he's saying to me is going in one ear and out the other." I could feel his pain, because I was having that same pangs of guilt for going against the natural order of things.

We had been sneaking around to see each other behind our parents back. It was something that I would never condone of Rebekah, but I couldn't exactly turn off the feelings that I had for Jacob. It was just one more obstacle that stood in our way. We had to find a way to rectify the situation or we would never be able to be with each other.

We had found this out of the way field, laid down a blanket and were now having a picnic with fried chicken and a potato salad that I made with pineapple. It's not something that I would normally make, but he did tell me that his favorite thing of all time was pineapple. I decided to incorporate it into the recipe. I had to make all of this under the sly, staying up late at night, while Henrietta slept upstairs having no idea what I was doing. I did have a little bit of company. Rebekah came down looking for something to drink. I gave her water and then I sent her back to bed with her sleepy doe eyes barely able to stay open.

"If we can't be honest with each other, Jacob, then we can't possibly be honest with our parents. They knew that we were involved, but I haven't spoken your name since they sat me down and had that talk with me. We really do have to find out what was so damaging to both of our family's that they would never talk to each other again. I've tried to dig into the *shtamm* history, but it hasn't been easy." I'd even turned to my Aunt, who was usually a wealth of information, but now wanted to remain neutral on the subject of the Millers and the Fishers.

He took a bite from the potato salad and his eyes lit up like the 4th of July. It made me happy to see that he was enjoying it and despite all that we had been going through, I was actually finding myself losing myself in the moment. In these brief seconds, I saw only bliss etched across his face. I had something to do with that.

"I don't mean to go off topic, but this is very delicious, Bethany. I've never even considered putting pineapple into a potato salad before. I'm not saying that the fried chicken isn't good either, but it really is the pineapple in the potato salad that makes this meal." He had picked up a drumstick, putting it up to my mouth and let me taste the batter. It was crunchy and just about the best thing that I've ever had in my mouth. I had my *maemm* to thank for that. Her recipes were ones that I had copied on several occasions.

"Bethany, I think that I'm going to start pulling out my hair, but for now, I think that we should just think of each other and not worry about what other people think. I would like you to reconsider about going on the humanitarian aid program. I think that it's the path that we have chosen and we can't allow anybody to get into our heads. I know that's hard and I know that you've all but made up your mind. I hope that our talk is helping you find a way to work past it." I felt totally at ease with him. That first kiss might have been chaste, but the next few were a little bit more passionate.

He was the perfect gentleman and he never tried to go any further than that. I think we both wanted a whole lot more. We never acted on those baser desires. We had been raised to wait for marriage to consummate the relationship. We had talked about marriage and even now Jacob was going to talk to the Bishop about getting a *zeugnis*. I wasn't so sure that it was a proper thing to do, considering that we couldn't get our loved ones to see eye to eye.

It was the perfect weather for a picnic. We were relaxing there and watching the formation of the clouds above our heads, holding hands and just not saying anything at all. The meal was sublime, but now it was time to relax and just enjoy each other's company. I loved the way that his fingers entwined around my own.

It was endearing the way that he constantly glanced over at me when he thought that I wasn't looking. I could see the love in his eyes and despite all the objections, we were deeply in love. We had to hide it from everybody else. Not even my friends knew about Jacob and he had kept the relationship completely hidden from his friends and *shtamm*.

"Bethany, I've had an epiphany and I don't think we're going to have to deal with this kind of interference any longer." I saw that something changed about Jacob. A resolve came over his features and it made me a bit panicked to think what he was going to do.

"I don't like that look. You better tell me what is going on in that head of yours."

He stretched his limbs, his shirt becoming untucked and then he realized his mistake and decided to tuck it back in. "Don't you worry about anything. I'll take care of it."

Chapter 7

I had just left Jacob, and finished my work for the day, including the laundry, which had piled up over the last couple of days. I was in the backyard hanging up the wash, when I heard raised voices. It seemed to be coming from inside the house. I couldn't believe that Rebekah and my mother in law would be sniping like that. I left the laundry out to dry with the sun in the wind doing what it was supposed to do . I was going to have to find out what was going on.

I went into the house from the back door and heard Jacob's voice as clear as day. "I've asked you both here including Henrietta to talk to you about what's going on between your *shtamm* and mine. I'm not leaving here until we figure this out. Your *dochtah* is too important to me to just let it go. So, either you tell me what's going on or we sit here and stare at each other for as long as it takes." I couldn't believe the gall of Jacob, who had come over here and summoned my *maemm* and father to some kind of meeting.

"My *dochtah* will never be with somebody like you. If I have to keep you away, then that is exactly what I'm going to do. I can't believe that you would think that coming to us like this would make any sort of difference." My *maemm* was standing, quite adamant and not about to change her mind. If anybody knew her, then they would know that when she had something in her head, there was virtually nothing that anybody was going to do to change her mind.

"My wife is getting upset and I think that you should leave before you make things worse young *mann*. This really isn't any of your business. If you think that you are going to emotionally blackmail us into talking to you about the past, then you are sadly mistaken. You will not have anything to do with my *dochtah*. If I hear any kind of rumor that you've been seen together, then I will have to step in and do something about it."

I didn't know exactly what my father was thinking, but I really didn't want to find out. He did have a temper when pushed into a corner. Unfortunately that was what Jacob was doing. My father was a pacifist like we all were, but that didn't mean he couldn't make our lives miserable.

Jacob stood defiantly. "I'm not going to stop seeing her and we are in love and plan to marry."

"That will happen over my dead body," my mother was steadfast to say. "When I tell you that my *dochtah* will not be seeing you again, then you can take it to the bank. Even if she is in love with you and I seriously doubt that, then she will abide by our wishes because we are her parents and she knows that she has to obey what we say. I think that my husband should have a talk with your father." Jacob had certainly stuck his foot in his mouth this time.

I stepped into the room to try to bring a little stability back into the proceedings, but it didn't look like that was going to happen.

My *maemm* put her arm around me and my father shielded me from Jacob, who was all but defeated. He had no idea how to fix what he had done. His attitude was that he was the *mann* and that he should be able to fix this. How could he possibly do that when he was making my parents uncomfortable and angry all at the same time.

"Bethany, tell your parents that we're going to be together whether they want me here or not." I felt totally trapped, unable to look at him in the eye and then hung my head in defeat.

"I think that you should leave. I believe that you've already said and done more than enough." I didn't mean to hurt him, but I had just met him and to break that bond of *shtamm* was not an easy thing to do. They had been there through all of my trials in life and had guided me with their hand with wisdom and discipline. I had to side with them for the time being, at least making it appear that way, but only because I didn't want to have yet another fight.

My mother had a death grip on my arm and stated emphatically "I think my *dochtah* has made herself very clear. She stands beside her *shtamm*. I think you should take a lesson from her. Maybe if your father was less inclined to let you run free, you might have more respect for your elders. This is the last time that I'm going to say this and I hope to *Gott* that you listen very clearly. Bethany is not going to see you anymore and she will not be going on this insane humanitarian aid program. I now see where she is getting these ideas. If it wasn't for you, none of this would be happening." I didn't like the way that my *maemm* was talking to Jacob, she was literally making him feel like he was 2 feet tall and not worth the effort to speak to any more.

Henrietta wasn't saying anything, but she was smiling and making me decidedly angrier by the second. If they were to push me any further, I might say something, but I managed to rein in my tongue.

"I'm going, but this isn't over by a long shot. I won't let you stop her destiny. Mark my words, I will find out what this rift is all about." My father came forward and placed his hand firmly against Jacobs shoulder. He then turned him and escorted him with no fight back to the door.

I didn't hear what he said to him, but I could see that it was having a profound affect. It made him glance over at me with this lost puppy dog look. I wanted to go to him and tell him that I was with him 100%, but to do so would only bring about a very fierce yelling match between me and my parents. I didn't want to go through that. Letting them think that I had backed down was my best course of action.

There was no way for him to get through to my parents, but maybe there was a way for me to get through to his. Surely, they would be more forthcoming and ready to listen to reason. They couldn't possibly be as stubborn as my parents. Why did it have to fall on Jacob's shoulder to make everything all right?

Chapter 8

I found myself rehearsing what I was going to say to his parents over and over again in front of the mirror. Sometimes I was more forceful and demanding and other times I was more meek and mild. I wasn't sure just which way to go, only that I felt that they would never toss me out the door like my parents had done to Jacob. I had seen Jacob's father in church, quite an imposing figure, but his mother was more staid and didn't say much of anything.

It would be nice to have parents like them growing up, but we all have to play the cards that we are dealt. It wasn't like I didn't love my parents, but I thought that they could be narrow minded and not willing to bend whatsoever.

I had taken my daily walk, not quite knowing if I was going to go through with this or not but then finally finding myself on their doorstep. I wasn't sure if Jacob was there, but I didn't hear his voice through the door. I was hoping that this could be something that would be between his parents and me.

I stood there for the longest time, looking at the door and then glancing back at the road and wondering if I should just turn around and go back the same way I came. I had brought some scrapple with me as a peace offering, something to get me into the door and hopefully to make a good first impression. I'd even packed some flowers, something colorful that would liven up their house. Swallowing hard, I brought my hand up to the door and hit the wood frame. It was like thunder in my ears. It felt like forever before somebody finally came to answer it.

The door opened. His *maemm* was standing there with flour on her hands. She ran her eyes up and down my body, most likely assessing the situation and trying to find the best way to deal with it. "I am..." she put her hand up to stop me, motioned me with one finger to follow her into the kitchen, which I did feeling like I was being called to the principal's office.

"I know who you are, Bethany. The only thing that perplexes me is the reason why you're here. I know it can't be anything to do with Jacob, because you were supposed to stop seeing each other." I was speechless; standing there with my hands folded in my lap, while I sat there at the kitchen table and waited for her to finish with what she was doing in the kitchen. "I know you must've come here for a reason, so why not just spit it out."

She placed the tea service in front of me, a beautiful set that most likely was passed down from one generation to the next. The tea was quite delicious and I looked at her over the top as I sipped it and wondered how I was going to say what needed to be said. I put the cup down, looking at her stern face, as she waited until I was courageous enough to say anything.

"I brought this." She eyed it with suspicion, picked up the scrapple and took a small section and sliced off two pieces for each of us. She got two plates from the cupboard, placed the white China onto the table and then sat down. "I hope you like it. I spent all night making it just for you." I thought that she would see that I was making an effort, but instead all I received was complete silence as a response.

I knew that her husband was the one that made the furniture. I had seen him selling it at the market when I was there selling my canned goods, not to mention blankets and scarves. He did make some remarkable pieces. I even had a China cabinet that came from his hand. Maybe that was something that I should mention in order to soothe the fearsome lady.

"I don't think that you could make a better scrapple than me, but by all means let's find out." I heard the sarcasm in her voice. She then took a bite and smiled. I thought for sure that I had done something right, but then she laughed in my face. She called me on the fact that I didn't use the right ingredients. "You must've been in a pretty big hurry or distracted, because this is nothing like the one I make. As for the flowers, you can take them with you, because I'm allergic." She wasn't sneezing, so I had to assume that this was just her way of slapping me across the face without actually doing it.

"I think that I might have made a mistake," I meekly said.

"Bethany, clearly you have. You thinking that you can come here with scrapple and flowers and hope to sway me to let you see Jacob was misguided. He's better than you. I don't want him even talking to you let alone having a relationship."

I thought for sure that my peace offering would be received kindly, but basically she had tossed it back into my face without even giving it a second thought. "If your parents had raised you right, you would know not to come here bearing gifts and hoping that things were going to change. I've always known that you Millers were a backstabbing lot, but I never imagined that you would sink so low as to come here with your hat in your hand." Once again, she had taken me by surprise, made it impossible to say anything at all without making me think that it was the wrong thing to do.

She had me shaking and my fingers were making the teacup spill the contents down the side. I put it down, placed my hands on the table and lifted myself onto my feet. It took a lot of effort just to do that. I felt totally outmatched and powerless to say anything in defense. I was trying to put myself in her shoes, but I would hope that I would have enough sense to at least listen to my *dochtah*'s argument.

"I'm leaving. I apologize if you took whatever I said as some kind of slight on you. It was never my intention to come here and make you angry. I see now that my coming here was a huge mistake." I backed away from her, because I really didn't want to turn my back on her in case she threw something at me. I didn't think that she would do something like that, but I had no idea what was going on in her head.

I stepped out into the yard, feeling like I would've liked to take all of that back, but unfortunately I had just done what Jacob did.

Chapter 9

We were walking on a path through the woods. Jacob hadn't said anything since he came to see me. I wasn't sure if he was mad at me or at his parents' or maybe it was a combination of both. I did see that he wanted to blow up, scream and yell and just let all of those frustrations just flow freely out into the open. Maybe it would do us both good that we screamed at the same time. I was too ladylike to do something like that.

"I was going to yell at you, but I know that your heart was in the right place. Did you really bring her flowers?" I nodded my head and he shook his vehemently like he couldn't believe that I had done something so foolish. "She was sneezing and her eyes were watering when I came home. I thought that she was upset with me, but then she sat me down and told me what you had done. At first, I came to your defense and I tried to make her see that you were just trying to do something nice to pave the way for us to be together."

"I imagine that didn't go over well." At least he was holding hands with me, making me feel like he was with me and not against me.

"Trust me, Bethany, I understand the sentiment, but you should've ran this by me first before you did that."

"Like your idea of going to my parents and ambushing them."

"I see your point, Bethany and I suppose that we were both just a little bit too pigheaded to realize that our parents would never listen regardless of what we said to them. If you have any ideas about how to go about this, then I am more than willing to listen." It was the first time that we had started to think together, not separately and going off half cocked with insane ideas that didn't amount to much of anything.

"Jacob, I don't know about you, but I don't think that we can do this alone. I didn't want to get him involved, but the bishop is privy to almost all the secrets in this district. Perhaps he can shed some light on this." Like I said, I didn't really want to get him into the middle of this, but he was the only one that I could think of that might be able to do something.

The trees were almost calling my name, the wind whistling through the leaves and knocking them onto the ground at our feet. They were a multitude of colors and I had to take a moment just to watch them lazily drift to the ground. We both looked at each other and knew exactly what had to be done.

The decision was made that we would talk to the Bishop. We were almost there anyway and before long we were standing with him outside, as he pondered what we had to say and listened with a careful and nonjudgmental ear.

"I'm glad you came to me with this. I thought that something like this might happen. I've been hearing things from the community and I didn't want to push the issue, but I thought it might be best that I talk to you both. I know that you have feelings for each other, but sometimes in life love is not always the answer. I'm not saying that you shouldn't be together, because I wouldn't put you in a position to choose between each other and your *shtamm*." He was dressed impeccably with a white shirt and black vest, his beard so long that it was actually fell the way down to his chest. He was stroking it absentmindedly, thinking about what to do and then he turned to us like a light bulb just went off over his head.

We listened to his idea and it was so simple in nature that it was almost foolproof.

I said with a bit of skepticism "I see only one problem with that plan. How do we go about getting them both into the same room at the same time? It's not like they're going to come willingly, especially if they know the other two are going to be there."

The Bishop had this look on his face "Bethany, let me take care of that. I just want you to be there when this all happens. I'm not going to promise anything, but your folks are reasonable adults. I'm sure that they just want the best for you. It's just that they are blinded by the past. It's time for them to put aside all that and finally say what they need to after all these years." He had told us that the rift was concerning a business deal that went sour.

Jacob said "What exactly happened?"

"It wasn't anybody's fault, but to hear each side, you would think that each one had sabotaged the other. Both of them were in business together. It was always known that Mrs. Fisher was the one that did all the cooking. Once that became public knowledge, people began to whisper that maybe she should go into business for herself. With the help of your father, Bethany, she did do exactly that. She became quite successful, but in the process she left behind the Millers. They never did get over that feeling of betrayal. That is what has been going on between them all these years."

Chapter 10

My *maemm* was the first to raise an objection "What's the meaning of this? Why have you called us here, Bishop?" My *maemm* and my Father were the first to arrive. They both saw the bishop and us standing together and knew that something was going on. "Don't tell me that they have elicited your help in this nonsense."

"For once, I agree with him and I don't think either one of us are very happy about being summoned here." This was Jacob's father, Jeremy, who has just arrived on the scene.

"Let's get something perfectly clear. I think that both of you care for your son and your *dochtah* enough that you will at least sit down in the same room together." The Bishop spoke with eloquence.

The bishop, Jacob and myself had arranged it so that there was a table between them. Jacob and I were both dressed in our Sunday best. We were really trying to put our best foot forward.

"If they can listen, then so can we." This was the stubborn streak of my *maemm*. We had made a little bit of progress, but there was still a whole lot more to do.

The Bishop continued "Jacob and Bethany have come to me with plans to marry. I've already given Jacob the *zeugnis*. He just needs your blessing to finally seal the deal. I think that after what is said that you'll see that they have nothing but respect for the both of you. This rift has been going on long enough. With my help, Jacob and Bethany have come up with a solution to the problem."

I said "I know that my *maemm* built a successful business by severing ties with you as partners. I think that was unfortunate. I've taken the liberty of signing over my rights to the business. I want the Millers to have my stake." I had just dropped a bombshell, and they were both taken aback by this latest turn of events. "I think this partnership was severed prematurely. If this is all that is keeping you from talking to each other, then I am glad to turn over my stake."

"You can't do that." My mother was quite adamant and was now standing with fire in her belly.

"I don't need your permission, *maemm*. I am an adult and I can make my own decisions. I would rather have Jacob than anything else and that includes being part of the *shtamm* business. I will still be in the business, but I will no longer have a partnership. Besides, I think we've been stagnant as of late. I know that Jacob's father has some connections that can get us into a few bakeries that have been untouchable." He was always going into town for fresh baked goods and building a relationship with the owners. That would come in handy to rejuvenate a business that had been stalled out for the last year.

It started them talking about the future and before long there was actually laughter instead of angry huffs.

Jacob piped in "I think that we have mended some fences here. I would like to have your blessing to get married. After that, we are going to continue our quest for humanitarian aid work. It's not that we're going to be gone forever but there's going to be a short period of time that we won't be around. We want you to know that we will always be in touch and that we will always be back. After all, Bethany has her *dochtah* Rebekah. She also has her loving parents and mother in law to think about. I have my parents. Now that this pettiness is behind us, I think that we can be one big happy *shtamm*."

In the next week, we were standing in front of all of our friends and loved ones in holy matrimony. We had a wonderful time with all of them, breaking bread and playing games with the young ones, until finally the bishop stepped forward. It was time to leave. We gathered whatever we had and put it into a horse and buggy. We said our goodbyes with a tearful Rebekah trying to hold onto me. She finally relented when I told her that I would bring her back a present.

When we reached the Airport, we both looked at each other and saw the huge airplane that was going to take us to Haiti. It would be the first time that we had ever been on an airplane. We were sitting on this plane, something that we had never been on before and about to take a journey that was primarily caused to the fact that both of us had the same path in life.

This had all started with me feeling something for Jacob and then dealing with the guilt of what my husband might think of this situation. I would hope that he would be happy for me and was now looking down on me with a smile.

Amish Crossroads Series

BOOK 2 – A love lost

Rachel H. Kester

Chapter 1

"I know that this has been a hardship on all of you, but I admire the strength that it took for all of you to come here today. We have a lot of work to do and each one of you has his assignments. This is going to be tedious, hard labor that is most likely going to exhaust you to the point that you can stand up at the end of the day. I know that we are asking a lot of you, but this is a joint effort by many other factions. I've already talked to father Jansen from the New England church. Along with his parishioners and volunteers, we will the working hand in hand with each and every one of them." I'd always admired the way that the Deacon could speak to a crowd. I hoped that I could emulate him in some way.

We landed in Haiti, a country that was hurting desperately. You could see the faces in the crowd that looked towards us with pleading eyes. As we arrived in Haiti, we were taken by bus, a monstrosity that spit out fumes that were going to destroy the earth one day. I think both myself and Jacob were thinking along the same wavelength. We both looked at each other and could see that neither one of us wanted to be on this contraption. Unfortunately, it was the only way to get to the outskirts and those that needed us the most.

"I don't know about you, but this is totally out of my element. I don't even know why I came here in the first place. My boyfriend decided for the both of us that we need to get away and do something meaningful with our lives. I guess I could see his point of view. We were wallowing in too much money and everything that we wanted. We saw the devastation that happened to this country and I think both of us wanted to make some sort of difference. Nicholas is my boyfriend and he's very good with his hands. He has built a few houses on his own." I didn't know why this woman was talking to me, but it felt nice to have a friendly conversation with somebody that wasn't from my own district.

I saw out of the corner of my eye that Jacob was talking to somebody as well. He was fine young gentleman with strawberry blond hair and muscles that seem to bulge out of his shirt like they were trying to escape the tight confines of the fabric. He had a big build, but you could see on his fingernails that they were dirty and that he had calluses on his hands from obvious hard work. We were sitting around this table in the center of this tent and enjoying whatever rations that came our way.

"I just got married myself and my beloved, Jacob and I decided that we both wanted to make the sort of difference that would leave a mark on the world. I've even convinced him to let me pick up a hammer. He's going to teach me the finer points of carpentry. I wouldn't even consider this back in my district, because it is frowned upon for a woman to do these type things." I don't know why I was unloading on this woman. I felt like we had this connection that went beyond just meeting for the first time.

She took a sip of her water and I could see that she was cringing slightly, but I couldn't understand why. Perhaps she had a sore throat that she was trying to keep from the others, in case that they would take her off the line and not allow her to help out anymore. "Nicholas has always been a good man, a catholic and he has been devoted to the community. I don't think I could ever love anybody as much as I do him. I don't think my family really understood the reason why we had to do this. It wasn't like we were just going to walk away and do nothing." I could see the conviction in her eyes, but there was something painful behind both pupils that I could see as vivid as day.

"Doing something like this really does take the toll. For the most part you feel this sort of elation from helping others." She was looking past me, almost dreamingly and it appeared to me like she was thinking something else entirely "I'm glad that we got a chance to meet. I've met some interesting people since being here, but so far nobody really has said much of anything. They are all caught up in their own little world and don't have time for chitchat. I always think there is time to smell the roses and you have to, because you only get this one life to live and then it's over." I didn't mean to sound maudlin, but doing what was right was something that I strived for every day.

I left behind my *dochtah* Rebecca, someone that was the light of my life and yet I needed to do this for myself. Jacob was from a *shtamm* that really didn't understand his desire to go off on this humanitarian aid work. I suppose I couldn't blame them, because really *shtamm* was the most important thing. We had done something that was unforgivable in their eyes. Thankfully, we had smoothed things over by the time we left for Haiti. They didn't particularly enjoy the fact that we were going to be away for days on end. They at least gave us their blessing and that was more than we could ever hope for.

I told her my name was Bethany and that I was from an Amish community. She snickered and pointed at me like she had known all along.

"I think I figured that out when you walked into the plane and looked around like you were in some sort of coffin on wheels. I was going to befriend you then and there, but you seem to have only eyes for the man that you were standing with. I can only assume that was Jacob. He was a great comfort to you as the plane took off. I found myself gripping Nicholas's hand, my fingernails digging into his skin and making him grimace with a sort of pain. I didn't mean to be like that, but I'm not the best flier. I sometimes feel that men should never have the capability to fly without wings." I felt the same way and there were moments up on that flight that I really thought that we were going to plummet to our death.

That was never more prevalent than when the plane began to rock. The pilot came on and told us that they were experiencing turbulence. I'd no idea what that was. I wanted to scream, but instead I kept my eyes focused on Jacob. It was the way that he kept me calm with a reassuring expression that made me feels safe. He was sitting over there with this young man. Amanda had gone and left the tent when my back was turned. I figured that I could at least find out what Nicholas was all about.

Something was bothering Amanda and I felt like it was my duty to at least be there for her. She wasn't really my friend, or maybe she was. I just didn't know.

Chapter 2

"Bethany, I want you to meet Nicholas. I told him that you want to learn carpentry. He told me that he would be willing to impart his wisdom on you. I think that between the two of us we might be able to show you the finer points. I'm not saying that you're going to understand it, but if anybody can, it would be you." I put my hand out in greeting and he took it by my fingers and gave it a kiss. I pulled away, feeling slightly guilty about having his lips on me. I turned to Jacob to see that he was not at all affected by that kind of affection.

"I'm sorry, I didn't mean to offend. I just wanted to let you know that it would be my pleasure to teach you carpentry. I don't know when the last time a woman wanted to learn something like that. I give you credit for wanting to do that. I think before long you'll be able to build your own house."

"Nicholas, the *haus* that I would like to build is on a parcel of land away from everybody else. There's plenty of acreage and there is a beautiful lake that surrounds the property." I don't know how many times I've thought about this particular desire. I've even seen a few pieces of land in the district that fit the bill. However, I still had the land that was left over from being a widow. I wasn't sure that I could just toss that aside for something new.

We all gathered outside to receive our assignments. When they told me that I was going to be giving out blankets, I protested vehemently. "I think that I would rather roll up my sleeves and get my hands dirty. If you don't mind, I think that I'm going to put myself in the hands of my husband Jacob and his new friend Nicholas."

"I don't know if I agree with this and it's a little unusual for a woman to pick up a hammer and nails. For this one time, I will make an exception. If you truly want to do this, Bethany, then I won't stand in your way." Deacon Alba was one of those rare individuals that saw everybody's point of view. I was glad that he relented and allowed me to learn something new. "I don't want you to get hurt, so please be careful and follow the directions to the letter." I was actually going to help build a *haus*, something that I had never done before but secretly fantasized about. Even my dearly departed husband had no idea that I felt this way. I'm not sure if he would understand even if he did.

All three of us were assigned together. Before long we actually had the sounds of hammering and sawing being the only thing that could be heard for miles. Little *kinner* came to watch as we worked our magic. I think that they were more interested in what Jacob and I were wearing than the actual accomplishment of putting something together with our own two hands.

I felt a tugging on my sleeve and I looked down to see this little one with beaming eyes looking up at me. He was African American, his hair as black as coal and he suddenly spoke with a French dialect that caught me a little bit off guard "My friends and I were wondering why you are wearing that." I could see their confusion. The other two that were with him came forward and was now standing waiting for an answer.

"I'm Amish and this is what we wear on a daily basis. If you want to learn more about my upbringing, then I would gladly tell you anything you want to know. I'm sure that you have questions. If you would allow me to finish up what I'm doing, then I might be able to tell you a story that would hopefully give you some insight into what being an Amish means. They seemed fascinated. I looked towards Nicholas and Jacob to see that they were commiserating together. I could see that they were friendly, jabbing each other with their hands and laughing when somebody hit their hand with a hammer.

Thankfully, that wasn't me and I was very careful and precise when I hit that nail with a hammer. I actually got a good rhythm going. I had about 10 boards completed and firmly secured. I felt great and I smiled, until Nicholas and Jacob were now standing right beside me. I was almost thinking that they were going to say that I was doing something wrong. They were smiling with pride and pointing to each other like they had something to do with it.

"I think your wife has got the knack of this. You certainly have a good one, Jacob. I only wish that Amanda would want the same things as the both of you do. I told her many times that I wanted to get married and have children. She has been very cold as of late. I don't know what the problem is; only that she doesn't seem like the same person that I met two years ago." I felt this instant liking for both Nicholas and Amanda and yet there was something underlying that was keeping them from being together.

There was a moment there that I thought about my *bobli* and I think I got a tear in my eye. Jacob was now hugging me and telling me that everything was going to be OK. I could see that Nicholas was a bit put off by this type of overt emotion. He was standing there uncomfortably, while we hugged it out and I finally got myself under control. My father and *maemm* were my lifeline and having them and *Gott* was always the three things that I held onto when I was away from them.

"We have two more *haus's* to make tomorrow and we're going to need all the *kaffe* that we can get our hands on." I saw Nicholas staring at the both of us. I got a pretty good idea that he was trying to make sense out of what we were trying to say.

"I don't mind hard *schaffe* and this experience has been more than I could ever imagine. I have the both of you to thank for that and don't think it was lost me the way that you were both so patient and calm while teaching me." I felt that they needed to know that I was grateful for their assistance. I think that I had a pretty good understanding on the subject of carpentry from the very beginning. It was like I'd taken to it like a duck takes to water. I had to admit that I enjoyed creating something with my own hands.

It was different from making sweaters and scarves. I think I found a calling that was unexpected. Nicholas and Amanda were struggling to remain faithful, or maybe there was something else going on that nobody was seeing. If I delved into this matter a little more deeply, I might be able to get to the heart of the matter.

Chapter 3

Meeting up with both Amanda and Nicholas for dinner was amazing. We actually got on like a couple of couples that had known each other for longer than a few days. For the first two days, we worked tirelessly and I actually found myself with callouses on my hands. It wasn't until the second day that we finally got up the courage to ask Amanda and Nicholas if they wanted to join us in our tent. There was nothing sexual involved and we made that point abundantly clear. When they arrived, we had already taken our meal to our tent. It had a bug screen that was keeping us from being bitten to death. We actually had to hold onto the opening of that tent, so that we could pull them into the interior without allowing any of the bugs to follow them in.

"I don't know about you both, but I'm getting a little fed up with all of these mosquitoes. They are everywhere. I'm just glad that during the day they seem to take a break from their blood sucking ways." There was definitely a weight hanging off of Amanda's shoulders. You could see that she was looking towards Nicholas and sighing deeply. Thankfully she was doing it so that Nicholas couldn't see what she was doing. I was the only one that was able to see the anguish on her face. I was going to have to get to the bottom of it one way or the other.

We sat down to what constituted a picnic. It was something that I was very equipped for and I had the necessary supplies to make a *scrapple*. I enjoyed the looks on their faces as they put the first bite into their mouth. It was like I had awakened all their taste buds at the same time. They consumed the entire meal without a single word being said around the supper table. It was a metaphorical supper table, but nonetheless we were breaking bread together and enjoying a few moments of peace during a tumultuous time.

"I've heard through Nicholas that you enjoyed using a hammer and nail. I don't mind saying that I've often thought about doing that myself. I'm really more of a take charge kind of girl. I would rather give out medicine and supplies. I hope that doesn't make me a bad person."

"Amanda, as long as your heart is in the right place, there is nothing that you can do that would be wrong. If you don't mind me saying, I think that you both coming here on the cusp of your relationship is amazing. You're not even married and yet you seem to know each other better than each of you can admit." I realize that I had made some sort of mistake, because I saw that Nicholas was now withdrawn. He was poking at his food with his fork, as if he didn't know what to do with it. "I hope I didn't say anything to ruin an otherwise wonderful evening together. If I did, please take my apologies for what they are and I hope that we can put this past us."

Nicholas couldn't even look me in the eye. He only glanced over at Amanda for a brief second before turning back to the meal at hand. As for Amanda, she was sullen, shifting in her seat nervously and tugging at the collar of her shirt like it was too tight on her body.

The rest of the night was uneventful. There really wasn't all that much said, except for some shop talk about what had to be done for the next day. Nobody wanted to talk about the elephant in the room. I knew that I had said something wrong when I mentioned that they weren't married. It was after all when they became so quiet that you could hear a pin drop.

"If you'll excuse me for a moment. I would like to get some air and then I'm going to return to my tent for the evening." I looked towards Nicholas to see what he was going to say. He shrugged his shoulders and apparently didn't want to get into any kind of argument. "I really do thank you for having us over." It appeared to me like she was biting her tongue with each word that was coming out of her mouth.

When she was gone, I turn to Jacob and nudged him on the shoulder to say something "Um, Nicholas, what exactly is going on between the two of you?" I don't know if I would've been so blunt. Now that he had broached the topic, it didn't seem like it was going to go away anytime soon. "I hate to get into the middle of this, but you both seem to be having problems."

"I don't know what her problem is. Ever since that I gave her the ring, she seems to be off. If she just wanted to tell no and throw the ring back in my face, then I would rather she do that, than become this cold creature." I wasn't sure that I could handle these kinds of words flying out of his mouth like venom. I got up and made a discreet exit.

Thankfully, the bugs had lessened slightly. They didn't seem to want anything to do with me in the first place. I walked over to the end of camp and I saw Amanda standing over by the river's edge with her hand outstretched on top of a branch to steady herself. As I got closer, I could see that she was shaking. She was sobbing very quietly. I knew that sound as well as I knew a chicken when it was laying an egg.

"I don't want to bother you. You seem to be upset and it might make you feel better to talk about it." I had my hand on my bonnet, making sure that it was staying on with this wind. She turned with her mascara running and her face showing the pain that was obviously causing her great discomfort. "I know that this has something to do with Nicholas. It is written all over your face as plain as day. I think that you would feel a whole lot better if you were to just say it. Once it's out there, it won't have any more power over you." I was doing my best to help her as best as I could, but I really did think that she needed to get this off her chest.

I saw the look on her face and it made me take a step back "Bethany, I appreciate your concern, but this is really none of your business. I don't like people telling me what to do and I don't think I have to tell you a damn thing. So, just leave me alone and stop prying into something that is my problem to deal with and not yours." Whatever this was that was bothering her, had her by the throat. There was nothing that was going to relinquish its hold without somebody coming to the rescue and giving her reason to say something that would make her feel better. "If you don't mind, I would really like to be left alone." I was just shot down. She made me feel like my help was a hindrance. I felt dejected. I went back to Jacob to see if he found out anything of use from Nicholas.

Chapter 4

It was two days later and I hadn't heard anything from Amanda. Any time that I came close to her, she would turn around and go the opposite direction. If that wasn't bad enough, being newly married, Jacob and I hadn't had time to be by ourselves for any more than a couple of hours at a time. We had barely enough time to consummate our relationship. That was after we had just got married. We had been so busy that we really didn't have time to do anything more than kiss each other good night.

"Jacob, I know that we've been very busy as of late and we haven't been able to find time to be together. Maybe we can make the most of it. The fact is, something is going on between Nicholas and Amanda and we have to get to the bottom of it. I think that between the two of us we can get through to the both of them." I had a ham sandwich in my hands. I took a bite and got the first taste of the bitter mustard within. It actually made me smile. I enjoyed this moment of peace between myself and my husband.

"I've already told you about his proposal and the way that she shot him down from the moment that he opened up his mouth. He finally convinced her to take the ring and give it some thought. Since then, she has been less than forthcoming. The one thing he doesn't understand is that she doesn't want to talk about it to him or to anybody. According to your own recollection, she has been very adamant about keeping this secret to herself." He wasn't wrong and I had done my best to try to draw her out, but she had been cold. It wasn't like she was even trying. It was almost like she had given up entirely on her relationship with Nicholas.

"I don't want to say this, but maybe there is another reason for her to be so quiet on the subject of his proposal. Maybe she's been seeing somebody else on the side and doesn't know where her heart lies. I know that might sound wrong on so many levels, but I know it is possible to love two men at the same time." He got this look on his face like I had been keeping something from him. I put my hand up to quiet any of his concerns. "I don't think you understand. My husband died and it didn't mean that my love for him died with him. I think that I'll always have a special spot my heart for him. I know you understand that, Jacob."

"I'm sorry; you just took me by surprise for a moment. I didn't realize what you were talking about, Bethany. It might be true but since you've already proven the concept, there is precedent for somebody falling in love with two men at the same time. It might even be that she suspects that he is the one that is stepping out on her. I think that if they both get the chance to talk openly and honestly together, they might be able to come clean with each other."

"Bethany, are you sure that you're not just interfering in their lives because our life is put on hold for the time being? I mean, you still have a *dochtah*. We both know that you've been thinking about her more often than not. Perhaps you need this as much as they need you. I don't think it takes all that much to figure out that you need something to fill that void. Don't get me wrong, I think that I have that same need." I hugged him, feeling comfort from having his arms wrapped around me. I sighed deeply and felt this warmth that made me feel like I was in the arms of someone that truly cared for me.

"I think that you might be the only person besides my *dochtah* that truly understands me. I always thought that I was alone after my husband died. I guess I was just waiting for my knight in shining armor to come calling. You were a bit of a surprise, but a welcome addition to my *shtamm*. I hope you know that there is nobody that could even hold a candle to you, Jacob. Trust me, if we had more time, I would be with you more often. I guess we have commitments that we have to make more of a priority. In the meantime, let's try to delve deeper into Nicholas and Amanda and see what makes them tick."

"I'll do what I can with Nicholas, but he is very hurt by all of this, Bethany. I'm not sure if he's going to be willing to talk. We both know that Amanda is a hard nut to crack. It's going to take some major patience on both of our parts to get through to them. I think that we can accomplish that. It's only because we have some experience in what it takes to be together when the odds are against you." We had overcome many obstacles, not the least being my own *shtamm* and his, coming to blows over a long past argument. It had been haunting them from the moment that they had gone into business together.

We could manipulate them and use our own experiences to our advantage. This was not something that was going to be easy by any means, but at least we had each other. I wanted more than anything to break through her defenses. This time I was going to go at it from a different angle. There was no point in trying to browbeat her into some kind of confession. I had to do more to fight the instinct to try to take over.

Chapter 5

I overheard Jacob talking with Nicholas. It didn't look like things were going according to plan. "Nicholas, I know the engagement is not exactly on solid footing. You can't let that stop you from being with the one you love. If I had stepped aside and did nothing when I was courting Bethany, we would never be together right now. Our *shtamm* would never be together today if I hadn't worked with my beloved to figure out a way around what was keeping us apart. What you need to do is try and…"

"I don't need your advice. I would rather you leave this alone. I know this might seem a little out of place, but this is a matter between me and Amanda. She doesn't feel like talking and I'm not going to try to force the issue. If and when she decides to tell me what's going on, then that will be on her and nobody else. Trust me, I've had arguments with her in the past and it's best to let things lie until she is able to figure things out on her own." This was not the way to do this. For him to do nothing was just going to exacerbate the matter even more.

"I think that you're wrong and I think…" he once again shut him down, stopping him in midsentence and keeping him from getting his whole thought out in the open.

"Jacob, I know that your heart is in the right place. I really think that this is Amanda's issue to handle. Have you ever thought that she just doesn't love me enough to want to marry me? Believe me; I've been thinking that over and over again for the past few days. It has kept me up at night. I toss and turn wondering if she is going to walk through that tent with some kind of explanation." He hit his finger with a hammer and made this cursing sound that made me want to clamp my ears shut with my hands. "I have to go get this looked at. When I come back, I don't want to hear this nonsense anymore."

I looked over at my husband. He shrugged as if to say that he had tried his best and failed. It didn't mean that he was going to give up by any means. That was not the way that our mind worked. We wanted to get to the bottom of this. The only way to do that was to go to the source of the problem.

I strolled over to find Amanda working the chow line and making sure that everybody was fed accordingly. I stood to the side and looked at her, until finally she glanced in my direction and said "I don't know how you do that, Bethany. It felt like I was feeling these two eyes bore into my very skull. I'm getting the feeling that you have something that you want to say. I also get the feeling that I'm not going to like it at all."

I convinced her to have a cup of *kaffe* with me and we sat down and looked at each other from across our cups "Amanda, I don't want to get into this again. I really think that you need to unload this burden that is weighing down your shoulders. Once you say it out loud, then you can finally put it past you. It can't be that bad that you can't work this out with your beloved." It appeared that I had struck a nerve. She reached over and grabbed my wrist for such determination that I felt like I was trapped in some kind of vise.

"I didn't want to get into this, but you just won't leave it alone. I do love Nicholas with all my heart. I don't want to be with anybody else but him, but that's not going to happen." She had me flummoxed. I couldn't understand what she meant by that and I was going to have to get more clarity.

"I see the pain in your eyes, but I don't understand where it's coming from. You say that you love Nicholas and you want to be with them, so why can't you just go to him and tell him that. Put the ring on and live the rest of your life together with happiness and love all around you." She was gritting her teeth. Her eyes were showing the same tears that I had seen when she was standing over by that tree the other day.

"I can't be with him, because I won't be around long enough to enjoy it. I found out about two weeks before I came here that I have an incurable brain tumor that is going to kill me. The only thing that I can take solace in is the fact that it will most likely be sudden and I won't feel very much pain when it does happen. Unfortunately, it also means I have a ticking time bomb in my head that is going to go off at some point. There is no surgery and I have been given a death sentence." I heard the words, but they seemed foreign to me and I felt like I was at a loss for words. "I hope now that you would leave this alone. If Nicholas comes by this information, then I will know where it came from."

I tried to make her sit down and talk to me about this, but she pulled away from me with such haste that she actually left fingernail marks along my arm. She didn't cry, but she stomped off in a huff. I couldn't blame her, considering the circumstances that were keeping her from being with the one person that she loved. It wasn't my place to tell Nicholas any of this. This was something that had to come from her own lips. I had to debate that issue, but I wasn't going to go through this alone. I was going to tell Jacob everything. He would keep it a secret and we might be able to work together towards a common goal.

Chapter 6

"I know that you mean well, Bethany, but are you sure that we should be trying to fix this? She doesn't have a whole lot of time left. She has been given a death sentence that can't be taken away. At some point, *Gott* is going to want her back to his side and there's nothing that anybody or anything, including the love of a good man can do to stop that. I think you can understand that more than anybody, Bethany. Maybe if you were to tell her your story, you might be able to get through to her." I'd never thought about that. Now that he had broached the topic, I felt that I was infinitely more prepared to help than I could even imagine.

"Jacob, I now know the reason why I'm married you. You have a good heart and a compassionate soul that reaches out to everybody that you come across. I'm going to go and find her and try to convince her with my own story. It's a good suggestion and I just hope that it makes a difference." I didn't want to rehash the old details of my husband's demise, but maybe his death would put things into perspective. If my story could help her to realize the truth, then maybe it was something that had to happen in order for me to help her. Everything happens for a reason. I think that the untimely demise of my husband was something that I had to go through in order to find true love again.

I didn't want to be that person, but I found a way to corner her on the outskirts of camp. She was now standing at the same tree that she was the other day. She seemed to find comfort here and then I noticed that she was holding something in the palm of her hand. It was the Bible and she was mumbling scripture underneath her breath and trying to find comfort in the words within.

"I think that's the best way to deal with this, Amanda. I've always been one to turn to the Bible for answers. You should listen to it and your heart. Neither one will steer you wrong."

"I told you that I didn't want to talk about this and you better not have told Nicholas any of this. I don't want him to know."

"Amanda, I think it's time that I finally told you my story. My husband died and I was left with a huge hole in my heart. It was just good luck that I was able to find some comfort in the Bible, not to mention my own *dochtah* Rebekah. I grieved for some time, until finally I was able to pull myself out of sorrow. It hit me like a ton of bricks. There were days that I couldn't even get up in the morning. I want you to know that you're not alone. This doesn't have to be a one woman army. You can rely on me and I will do what I can to help you."

"You just won't give up. I will say that your story did make me think, but now I need to ask you a question. If you had to do it all over again, would you have married him, even if you did know that he was going to die in the next year? Be honest with yourself and then you can be honest with me." She had definitely caught me by surprise. I didn't know quite what to say. I'm not sure if there was a right answer or a wrong answer.

"If I were to be truly honest, I would say that I would never want to give up those moments that I had with him for anything in this world. I think that I might have spent more time with him, but that's what anybody would say in my shoes." I had gotten her to talk, but now it was up to her to decide if she wanted to make that leap of faith.

"I hear what you are saying, but I doubt that he would have thought the same thing. If he had known that he was going to die, he would never have pursued you in the first place. I think that you just gave me my answer." I didn't like the sound of that. She looked like she had just made a decision that was going to change the rest of her life "I think I know exactly what I need to do. This is no time to get married. I need to do this on my own and I can't have him hovering like some kind of nursemaid. Once he finds out, he's going to treat me like I am some kind of broken doll. Each time that I cough or sneeze, he will be thinking that this is the end. How can I put him through that and live with myself?"

She walked away from me and I felt a compulsion to follow. She went directly to her tent. I could see through the flaps that she was looking for something. When she found it, she raised it to the air and I could see the shining sparkle of the diamond. It wasn't ostentatious by any means, but it was a symbol of their love. I couldn't wear one myself, but I understood the sentiment of something that would cement their bond for all time. I thought for sure that she was ready and willing to except the proposal, but then she stepped out and I knew that I was definitely barking up the wrong tree.

"Amanda, you don't have to do this. We can talk more and look to the Bible for the answer."

"Bethany, your story did inspire me and my love for Nicholas makes it necessary for me to walk away from this." She held the diamond ring in her hand and she walked over to where Nicholas was now busily hammering and putting up drywall.

He stopped all motion, like he actually knew that she was there and then turn to see the diamond ring in her hands. His elation was short lived, as she walked up to him and tossed the ring into his chest.

"I can't marry you and this relationship is over. I want you to have the ring back. Get whatever money you can for it or keep it and give it to some other girl that is more worthy. I don't care what you do, but you need to leave me alone." She had not only thrown the proposal back in his face, but had essentially stripped away the relationship that they did have.

Nicholas was tongue tied. He couldn't speak and all he could do was stare at her. I think he was hurt beyond words. There was no going back from this and she had taken this step without thinking about the consequences. I wanted to grab her and shake her, but I didn't.

She turned to me and said "Now, are you happy. I'm giving him the ring back and he has no reason to come after me anymore." It was bad enough that she had given back to ring, but it was nothing compared to the expression on Nicholas's face. He was floored. When he tried to reach out for her, she pulled her shoulder back when he made contact.

Chapter 7

It had been a whole day since we had seen Amanda. When we went to look in on her, we found that she had left in a hurry. There was nothing other than a few pieces of discarded clothing that were left behind. I felt bad that I had put her into that position. It wasn't my place to force the issue. It was my way of helping, but it was to no avail. She had done something rash and now she was going to run away from her problems.

Jacob and I were back at it and I was getting a healthy dose of reality when I looked over at Nicholas. He was staring daggers at me. I think he knew that I had been responsible in some way. I wasn't exactly hiding it with my head bowed down in shame. "I think that you should talk to him, Jacob. He's like a *bruder* to you and I know that is something that you have secretly harbored. Being from a *shtamm* with no siblings, I can imagine how his friendship would mean the world to you." He had its sleeves rolled up and he looked me and smiled, before making his way over to Nicholas.

There was no way that I was going to miss this. I made a point of being close to them, so that could listen into what was being said.

"Nicholas, I know that must've hurt, but you have to go to her." It didn't look like he was getting through and Nicholas was pounding the hammer even harder. Most likely to drown out everything that was being said to him "I don't like being ignored." I could see the anger welling up inside of Jacob. His face was flushed and he was getting the silent treatment in return. "I think you have to go and talk to her." His voice was getting a lot louder. "For *Gott* sakes, you don't know what's going on." I could sense what he was going to say before he did it and yet there was no way that I could stop him. "She's dying of an incurable brain tumor and you are acting like an ass."

I went over and put my hand on Jacob's shoulder. He looked back of me and realized that he just made a mistake. I shook my head, indicating that it was not his secret to tell.

"I knew that she was sick, but I didn't know how bad it was. I told her that it didn't matter, but she still wasn't ready to talk about it. I know that your heart is in the right place, Jacob but this is really none of your business. It's not any of yours or that meddling wife of yours either. I'm sure that this would have blown over and she would've come to me in time. You both have made things worse by trying to make her talk before she was ready. I don't want to hear anything more and I'm tired of beating my head against a brick wall." It was a different analogy and I was a little confused by the statement, but then I got the idea behind it.

"My husband didn't mean anything by it and you just flustered him to the point that he blurted out something that wasn't his place to say. Now that it's out there, you can go to her and tell her that you understand. That's all she wants and believe me I know how a woman's mind works. Just show her some compassion, listen to what she has to say and then go from there. I'm not saying it's going to be easy, but we'll be with you every step of the way." I saw the same look of disdain that he had just shown Jacob now directed towards me.

"I just finished telling your husband that I don't want his help, I don't need his help and I certainly don't need you telling me what to do. Leave me alone and stop getting into the middle of something that is none of your business. We both know that you can't help yourself, because it's in your DNA to try to fix things. I know all about the Amish and at first I thought it was cute, but now it's starting to get on my nerves." I could see that he wasn't going to listen to reason. He had turned his back on us and was now pounding that hammer even harder than before.

I tried to tug on his sleeve, but he pulled away and glared at me with hatred in his eyes. I had ruined his relationship and what could've been fixed was now broken beyond repair. I wanted to do something, but I had no idea how to find Amanda, let alone get through to her. I just figured that if I had the chance to speak to her directly again that I might be able to make her see that not everything was as bad as it could be. She could still have a life with Nicholas, albeit a short one, but why not grab onto whatever life can give you.

I took Jacob by the hand and we walked away from him. I could see that Jacob was feeling like he had just lost his best friend "I don't know what to do for him. I tried to reach out, but my hand was basically slapped away. I suppose I can't blame him for his reaction. How can he possibly walk away from the love of his life like that?" He did have a valid point, but it was not my place to have the answer.

"I think that we've done more than enough and we should just leave this alone." It was my way of trying to backpedal, but frankly I wasn't going to give up without a fight.

Chapter 8

I told Jacob that his losing it in the heat of the moment had caused the rift between him and his friend. He was as stubborn as ever and I saw the Jacob was willing to work alongside Nicholas, but he wasn't able to defend himself. Nicholas didn't want to talk at all. It left me with a very difficult decision to make.

I still had it in my head that I could get Amanda to talk to me. I couldn't do that with her disappearing like that. It didn't feel right to invade her privacy, but I saw no other choice. I went over to Amanda's tent, making sure to lift up my long plaid skirt, so that it wouldn't drag across the dew covered ground. It was just lucky that nobody had been assigned that tent. Apparently they had no idea that she was missing in the first place.

I put my hand through the flap, look back to see if anybody was watching and then I went inside. There wasn't much left. The discarded clothing was the only clue that she had ran off in haste. I found a matchbook in a blue blouse, looked at it and saw that it was from a neighboring bar that we had passed on the way into the encampment. It was quite the wonder that Deacon Alba or even Father Jansen didn't have a clue that she was gone. I had heard Nicholas say that she wasn't feeling well. For the most part he was trying to keep this under wraps for as long as possible.

As I was leaving the encampment, I snuck past both Father Jensen and Deacon Alba. They were both deep in thought and conversation about the Bible. I could hear that they were having a heated debate over which Bible was more accurate. I used that distraction to get out onto the road. I felt the heat of this tropical setting making my clothes stick to me like a second skin.

I showed the matchbook to several locals. There was one child that had long stringy dreadlock hair that decided to take pity on me. "I know exactly where that is, but it's no place for a lady like you. I gave him a bit of money. It sealed the deal and he was happy to oblige. He even offered me a bicycle and I took him up on his offer. We rode in silence and then we came across the bar in question.

There was no signage and it was just a hole in the wall. I heard what sounded like laughter coming from inside. I open the door and the first thing I smelled was stale beer. If that wasn't bad enough, the body odor was significant and it hit me like a ton of bricks. I looked around and then I saw Amanda waiting on the tables.

I put my hand on her shoulder and she looked back at me with a smile. That soon faded when she realized who it was. "I don't know why you can't just leave me alone."

"Amanda, I came here in good faith. I brought you something that might help you." I took out the Bible from underneath my clothing. I opened it to a particular passage. "There is a fable that mentions a man walking in the sand with two footprints. One of his own and one of *Gott* following him. When he is at it his lowest, he looks to see that there's only one set of prints. He asked *Gott* why he left him. *Gott* tells him that he has never left him. When he was at his lowest, he carried him on his shoulders. I want you to let him do the same thing for you." She was staring at me. I thought for a moment that she was going to come back with me, but then she changed.

"I see what you're saying, Bethany, but this doesn't change anything. I'm still going to die and no words from the Bible are going to make a bit of difference. You came a long way for nothing. I would suggest that you turn around and go back the same way you came."

"Don't you think that Nicholas deserves the respect of allowing him to decide what is right for him?"

"I will always love Nicholas. If I were to allow him to make that decision, then I would put him through a hell that nobody should have to go through. I just can't do that. I don't know how many times I have to tell you this before it gets through that thick skull. I want the best for him and I'm not it." She was adamant. Her voice had raised an octave. It was a little too loud for my liking. The three patrons that were in the place had taken avid interest in what we were saying. It was almost like they were on the edge of their seats to hear what was going to happen next.

This wasn't going to work and I needed reinforcements in the form of Jacob and Nicholas. I don't think I was going to be able to get her to see that love was always worth the risk. I needed Nicholas to show her that there was still time to enjoy each other.

Chapter 9

"I know you don't want to, Jacob but I think it's best for everybody. We can't allow them to stay apart, especially when they are so much in love. We've gone too far to turn back now. You need to talk to him. This time I will be more than happy to stand with you. I think together we are a formidable team." I should've realized that before, but all I could see was what I thought was right. I need to find out if Nicholas was really that much in love. If he was, then I could use that to get him to fight for the one he loved.

"Not you again. I think I made myself clear the last time." Nicholas was alone at the edge of camp and it was quite amazing to see that he was in the exact same spot that I had seen Amanda. "I come here to be close to her."

I sat down, seeing that he had a pair of earphones in his ear. There seemed to be music coming from within. I had been seeing all of these technological wonders from the moment that we entered onto the plane. Cell phones, laptops and even MP3 players were the order of the day. I was not going to get caught up in that technological trap, but it didn't mean that I wasn't curious. I pulled myself from those thoughts and turn to more important matters. "Nicholas, how much do you love Amanda?" I had knelt down and was now touching his hand. Jacob was standing to the other side.

"I don't even know how to answer that. I just know that I am nothing without her. She makes me feel like I can be a better man. I love her with all of my heart and soul. There's nothing that could tear us apart and yet she is doing that all on her own. I don't want to be without her. I understand that she feels that she has to do this alone. She doesn't want to hurt me by her untimely demise, but I don't think that's her decision to make."

I'd gotten my answer and it was exactly what I had suspected all along. "I think you have to tell her that. She needs to hear it from your own lips. I know that this is hard, but rest assured that Jacob and I will be with you. You don't have to accept our help. It's there if you need it." This time, we weren't browbeating him into anything and we were showing him that his choice was clear.

His answer came in the form of his head nodding. I slapped Jacob on the arm to get his attention. This time we talked to Father Jensen and Deacon Alba and they both agreed that they would allow us a short furlough to find her.

When we came onto her doorstep, she opened the door and almost smashed it back in my face. It was Nicholas who put his foot against the jam, preventing her from doing so. "I think we need to talk. I love you Amanda. I didn't know how much until these two came along and opened up my eyes. I know that we don't have a whole lot of time, but I think that we should be together. I know that I am nothing without you." This seemed to be softening her resolve. She opened the door and let us enter.

It was a small apartment over the bar with very little furnishing. We sat down and I opened the Bible. We began to work through everything that she was going through with the help of the good book

"After reading the Bible and listening to what you have to say, I now know that I was being selfish. It was never my intention. I was hurting you more than I can ever know by keeping you at arm's length. If you truly want me, then I would like to accept your proposal." It was a far cry from what she was feeling the other day, but at least we had done something good.

Chapter 10

There didn't seem to be any reason to wait to get married. When she accepted the proposal, they went to Father Jensen for his approval. He listened very carefully to what they had to say. Then he asked them questions and then gave them his blessing.

The wedding was almost exactly the same as the one that Jacob and I had. There were a few details that were left out of our ceremony. We didn't have rings to share with each other. We didn't need that bond to cement the love that we had for each other. Our souls were forever entwined and there was nothing that was going to tear us apart. We listened to them profess their love for each other. It ended with a tearful kiss at the end.

"It's my great pleasure to announce the marriage of Nicholas and Amanda." There was a rumble of applause from those that were in attendance. This included the locals, who were more than happy to supply whatever food they could do without. Even a hunter from a nearby village came with a goat. He had prepared this delicacy that everybody seemed to enjoy.

"I don't know what we would ever have done without you in our lives. We apologize for being pigheaded, but this was very hard on the both of us." Nicholas was now speaking from the heart and it made me feel good to think that we had given them hope. "I'm not giving up on Amanda. I've heard of some work that is being done in Europe that might be of interest. Amanda has agreed to fight and we have you to thank for that."

"Nicholas is right and I had all but given up. I don't know what the future holds, but I do know that I will spend it with Nicholas. Who knows, we may even find a cure for the tumor. I have decided to think outside the box. I've reached out to some holistic healers." I had suggested the very same thing. I never did go in for medicine. I always thought that the body was its own cure. That being said, I also knew that our time on this earth was limited.

After the feast, we followed them to the airplane. They gave us big hugs and told us that they would never forget us. We turned to each other. I think Jacob and I were thinking the same thing. We may not ever know what happens with them, but we had done a remarkable thing.

His hand found mine and I knew that our path was meant to cross with that of Nicholas and Amanda. I just had to wonder what other fires we were going to put out with the word of *Gott*.

Rachel H. Kester

BOOK 3 – A strained faith

Rachel H. Kester

Copyright 2015 © Rachel H. Kester

All right reserved

Chapter 1

We were waiting for the Bishop to address us and we hadn't had time to do much of anything lately other than work our fingers to the bone. Jacob was holding my hand. I was looking lovingly into his eyes, knowing full well that we probably wouldn't be able to be together later in the evening. We've been here for about two months and our time in Haiti was rapidly coming to an end. We'd only been together one time in all that time. I think it was the anticipation of the moment that made it that much more special.

"I just want to tell you, Bethany that your work over the last few days has been nothing short of remarkable. We've been so busy lately and with Nicholas and Amanda jumping ship, we have been even busier. I just want to take this time to thank you for your hard work. I've never seen anybody take to carpentry like you do." It was nice to hear him say that. The only praise that I had been given recently was by the locals. There were always coming by with fresh fruit or some foods that they had made specifically for us when we were on the job.

The Bishop finally arrived, and you could literally hear the hushed whispers of everybody as he made his way to the front of the crowd inside this tent. I wasn't much for camping, but this experience had been quite the eye opener. I could live off the land easily. My father had been very diligent in making sure that I had survival skills growing up.

"I want to thank all of you for coming in here on such short notice. I'll make this brief. The next wave to come through here will be here sometime in the next few days. We don't have a set timetable and it might be longer than we expected. I know you all have loved ones waiting for you to come home, but these things are unavoidable. I just want to make one mention of Bethany and Jacob."

At the mention of our names, Jacob and I look towards each other and then towards the Bishop "Nicholas and Jacob are the finest two carpenters that we have ever had. Unfortunately, Nicholas had to take a leave of absence. I think we all know the circumstances that surrounded that decision. I just want to say that Bethany has more than made up for his absence." It was the best I was going to get. As everybody filed out, people were congratulating me for a job well done and patting me on the shoulder.

There was only one person inside the tent that really wasn't paying attention. It was the lone doctor for this district. Nobody really knew much about him. He was quite gifted when it came to medicine. What we did notice was that when we were having services on Sunday, he was reluctant to attend. We did know that he was a devout catholic and the rumor mill was abound with a mention of something that had happened to him that had seriously tested his faith.

He was still here inside the tent, but he wasn't paying attention to anybody but the file in front of his eyes. He was mumbling something underneath his breath; He was scribbling notes that looked like cat scratchings to me. "He is showing improvement, but I am wondering if there are any underlying conditions in his family that might make sense of his illness." I couldn't help but to overhear him. He had a tendency to talk out lout to himself as if nobody else was around him.

"Excuse me doctor, but I was wondering if there is anything that you need." I saw him stop. He made this huffing sound like I was disturbing him and then he looked up to me with this unamused smile on his face. "I just saw that you were preoccupied and I was wondering if you had a chance to have anything to eat this morning?" In all the days that I had seen him, I had never seen him eat anything. It didn't mean that he didn't, but for some reason he just didn't want to partake with the rest of us.

"Young lady, I am perfectly fine and I can take care of myself. I don't need a hen mother over my shoulder, trying to make me eat my vegetables and wash my hands." He was arrogant; not very pleasurable to be around and frankly everybody was doing everything they could to avoid him. The number of accidents had vastly diminished and anybody that was hurt was reluctant to go to him for assistance.

"There's no reason to get defensive. I was just trying to be nice. I don't know what your problem is, but maybe you should try to make friends."

"I don't have the luxury of making friends. My job is to keep everybody healthy, so that they can continue to work until the next wave of volunteers show up. Have you ever thought about the fact that most of you are temporary at best? I've been here for two years. I am perfectly happy being by myself." He lifted his 5 foot nine frame, smoothed down his blue shirt and then walked away with an air of confidence and conceited genius around him.

"I wouldn't bother trying to talk to him. Nobody else does. I know that we are supposed to be friendly with open arms, but he really does make it difficult to do that. Bethany, you might be the only one that has talked to him since we've gotten here, unless of course you're injured and had to tell him where it hurts." I've heard through many sources that his bedside manner was atrocious. It was more clinical than caring. He believed that he was a *Gott* among men and that he could play *Gott* because he had the lives of all of us in the palm of his hands.

I was getting used to strapping on the tool belt, picking up the hammer and walking out into the morning sun with the express purpose of yet again building another house. In the two months that I had been here, we had already made significant progress in everybody's lives. A dozen houses had been built with these two hands. I did have a remarkable support system with my husband Jacob and several other workers that really didn't know the word quit. They had the same kind of mentality when it came to work that Jacob and I did. That was very hard to reason with.

Chapter 2

"Bethany, I'm going to be on the other side of the house. I'm giving you the duty of keeping everybody moving." With Nicholas gone, Jacob had taken on the role as a leader. It's not something that was surprising in my book. I would say that I was very proud of him. He had shown me that his leadership skills came from being an example to everybody else. He was the first one to the site every morning with me standing by his side. We were at least an hour into the job before anybody else had shown up.

"I'll do what I can, Jacob but they really do listen to you." Being a woman, it was hard to get people to respect me, but I had been making inroads with everybody that I worked with. They were quite amazed to see that I had skills. I've never had any formal training to speak of. If I wanted to, I could've worked through the night. I would never lose the momentum that I had at the very beginning of the day. "Jacob, I just want to say that I love you." He turned and embraced me and whispered the same exact thing into my ear. We hadn't gone even a day without saying it. We had promised that even in anger that we would never go to sleep that way.

Jeremy, a young man of 20 years old had a carpenter's apprenticeship. Instead of honing his craft someplace else, he had decided that he wanted to make a difference. "Bethany, I don't normally ask for help, but I've seen you on several occasions and I think that you could give me a few pointers." He showed me his difficulty. It was an easy fix that had him well on his way to becoming quite proficient with a hammer. If it was anybody else, I would think that they were just trying to get close to me, but he already had a fiancée that was a nurse practitioner working 12 hours a day seven days a week.

"I think you've got it, Jeremy. You might have the same kind of acumen to this profession that I do. It's like you were born to pick up a hammer and build something with your own two hands." I'd always been creative, but my claim to fame was my clothing and the cane goods that I had sold at the market. I do have to admit that since my husband had died, I had to pick up the slack and do a lot of the things that a man would do. That included patching a hole in the roof.

I heard a commotion and then somebody screaming for help. I ran to see what was going on and I saw that

Jacob was pinned underneath a pile of rubble. If that wasn't bad enough, the boards that were on top of him had nails. Everybody was gingerly pulling them away from him, but they had already punctured his upper arms and he was bleeding profusely. I acted quickly, grabbing a drop cloth and putting it over the wounds. I applied pressure, as we moved hurriedly towards the medical tent.

"Put him on that table over there." William was the Dr. in charge and was already getting everything prepared for the wound. He disinfected it, making my husband Jacob cringe, but he showed no signs that he was going to scream out in agony. "I give you credit. Most people in your position would be begging me for some kind of pain killer. You're the first in a while that hasn't been a baby about these things." He had cleaned the wound, sanitized it with alcohol and was now suturing those cuts so that they could be bandaged.

"I appreciate everything you're doing... but I would like to get back to work as soon as possible." Of course Jacob would be hell bent on getting back on to his feet too early. It didn't look like the Dr. was going to have any of it.

"I'm afraid that that's impossible. I'm going to need to keep you here for at least a couple of days to monitor your condition. Those wounds are not going to heal without proper rest and medication." He was very staid, his speech monotone like he was some sort of unfeeling robot.

"I'm sure that with prayer and the guidance of *Gott* that I will be able to heal quickly."

He actually snickered at Jacob "*Gott* has nothing to do with it, unless you are implying that these two hands are Gott like. I'm the only *Gott* around here. As for the one that you pray to every Sunday, I have to say that he has been doing a very poor job of it lately." I could hear his cynicism, his lack of faith and his desire to make everybody around him as miserable as he was. "If *Gott* is so almighty, then why do bad things happen to good people?"

"You have to know that *Gott* does work in mysterious ways." Jacob was trying to get through to him. It was like trying to reach something through a brick wall. He wasn't having a whole lot of luck. I would say the doctor felt that *Gott* had forsaken him in some way. "You just have to have faith."

"Young man, the only faith I have is in medicine and in the skills that I have been taught over the years. I don't need to look to a deity for guidance. In my mind there is no such thing." Whatever had destroyed his faith must've been something monumental for him to step away from the light of the Lord.

"I'm sorry, but I've been sitting here and listening to all of this and I just can't take it anymore. Your whole idea that *Gott* is nothing makes me feel sad for you." He turned to me with glaring eyes and I saw the anger and what could only be resentment hitting me like a ton of bricks.

"I think I changed my mind. If you really want to leave, then by all means go ahead and see if your *Gott* will protect you from your sutures being ripped open." He was really getting on my last nerve. Jacob was about to take him up on his offer, but I put my hand on his chest to keep him from moving.

Chapter 3

Jacob was out of commission for the time being, but work still had to be done. I couldn't afford the luxury of staying by his side all the time. I was going to have to continue the mission at hand. He would want me to do this. He all but tried to push me out of the tent before I became a nuisance to the doctor. I was this close to confronting him, sitting him down and outlining the reasons why he should be holding onto the cross with both hands.

As I was leaving, he looked at me "*Gut*, I'm glad that you're leaving because I can't stand to listen to you any longer. You speak of *Gott* like he influences your decisions every day, but what has he done for me lately? I've been a loyal servant to the Lord and yet he takes away the one thing that I cherish the most. He took away my... Never mind, I need to get back to work. I could see that he was about to confess something, but at the last second he had decided to pull back before he went too far.

"Doctor, don't think for one second that this is over. I'm going to get to the bottom of what's bothering you. Then you can put it past you and look towards a better future." His hand gripped my wrist so hard that I thought he was going to break it.

"Young lady, your whole mentality about *Gott* is skewed. If you truly looked at what he has done for mankind, you would know that it was nothing compared to what these two hands do every day. People pray to him for patience and mercy, but sometimes all they receive is silence. How can a *Gott* that looks down on us from above be so judgmental? How can a *Gott* like that be somebody that I can worship?" This was very hard and I could sense that there was an underlying reason for all of this. It had something to do with his loss, but so far he had been less than forthcoming about what that was.

I returned to work thinking about William and how he had been so jaded about *Gott* that he was looking towards his own work and his own hands as something that everybody should bow down to. I will admit that his expertise working on Jacob was professional but detached. He moved with grace and determination. He never gave up until all those wounds had been stitched and he was now resting comfortably.

The fact that he had just done that for my husband made me want to help him find his way back into the light. I knew that I couldn't force him, but maybe I could get him to open up enough that I would be able to try to make sense of why he was feeling this way.

"Bethany, your husband was amazing. He jumped in front of that kid like his life was nothing compared to the one that he was trying to save." I had heard inklings of his heroic nature, but I was too caught up in getting him to medical attention that I wasn't paying much attention. "That kid was going to be crushed underneath that debris. He pushed him out of the way at the last second." As Jeremy told me the story, I could almost envision it in my head. He was a good man. He would do the right thing and even if that meant putting his own life on the line.

At the end the day, I went back to the medical tent. I stuck my head into the opening to see that the Dr. was nowhere to be seen. I saw Jacob sleeping soundly. I sat down and put my hand on his hand. He blinked his eyes open, saw me sitting there beside him and smiled. "I'm sorry, but I'm not really going to be much company tonight." I didn't care about that. I was going to stay by his side until morning.

"You can't be here." William had returned and was now standing over me like he was judge jury and executioner. "I don't allow anybody to stay overnight." He was quite adamant, but I stood my ground and held onto Jacob's hand in a death grip. "Fine, do what the hell you want, see if I care." I didn't want to make him anymore upset than he already was. There was no way that I was going to leave Jacob in the condition that he was in.

I snuggled close to him and we drifted asleep. Before I did close my eyes, I saw William looking over at us and I thought for a brief moment that there was a small smirk at the corner of his mouth. Maybe he was human after all. It would be interesting to see if there's really anything that I could do to help him. The first thing I needed to do was to find out what was eating him up inside. He was popping antacids like they were tic tacs and I could see that he was favoring his right leg more than his left.

He had been trying to hide it from the moment that we arrived. There were times that his concentration on keeping his injury to himself became quite known. I think what ever happened to his leg was affected by his emotions and the way that he interacting with others. I think everybody deserves happiness and that wasn't any more apparent than this man that was wallowing in self-pity. I don't know why it meant so much for me to make him see the error of his ways. I wasn't going to stop until I found a way to get through that tough exterior shell once and for all.

Chapter 4

"What the hell do you mean that you can't find him?" It was his voice that awoke me from a dead sleep. I rose up to see that he was now arguing with a small child. "I gave you enough money to choke a horse with and you told me that you could get results." The kid was speechless, almost panic stricken and looking at him with fear in his eyes. "I don't want excuses. I just want you to go out there and find him." I wanted to intervene, but I was still half asleep. He was visibly shaken and he was holding the kid's shoulders with such determination that I thought for sure that he was going to shake him until he fainted.

"I'm sorry, but I talked to everybody I knew. You have to understand that these things take time." I had been around the block a few times with the locals. I could see that this kid was one of those that liked to use people for their money. There are only a few chosen ones that could really be trusted to look for information on your behalf. This was not one of them. This kid would sell you a bill of goods and leave you thinking that he had done you a favor. "Maybe if you gave me a few more dollars. I might be able to pry some information from those lips that remain sealed." He was now trying to pump him for more money, but I didn't think that the Dr. was going to take the bait.

"Get out of my sight. I never want to see you again." The kid shrugged his shoulders, but then saw something in the doctor's eyes that made him turn tail and run like a scalded dog.

I got up and went over to where William was now bent over holding onto his forehead and literally shaking with rage. I put my hand on him and he instantly became all tense, but he didn't try to push me away. "Doctor, he may not be the right person to talk to."

"Bethany, I don't know what it is, but people are not exactly friendly around here." It probably had something to do with the way he spoke down to people. He made them feel like they were inferior in some way. "I just want to find my father." Now we were getting to the meat of the situation and maybe if I just listened he would open up on his own. "I've already lost my mother to a drunk driver and it gave me this limp as a permanent reminder of that fateful day." So, his whole reason for being here was finding his father. At the same time he was acting on behalf of the locals to give medicine and anything else they needed to keep healthy.

"I think I might be able to help." He looked to me incredulously, smiled like I was telling some sort of joke and then turned his back.

"I don't think that will be necessary, young lady." He did know my name, but he insisted on calling everybody young lady or young man. I think it was just his way of not personalizing his approach to medicine. He didn't want to become emotionally attached. That was a trait that was needed in his profession. He couldn't have his heart on his sleeve, because he would be a basket case with every patient that he lost.

"Let me talk to a couple of locals. They aren't exactly friendly to foreigners. If you didn't know already, most people don't like you in the first place. They try their best to be safety conscious, just so that they won't have to be subjected to your bedside manner."

"Bethany, leave him alone and let him get back to what he was doing." Jacob had now struggled to his feet, leaning on the bed frame of each individual bed in front of him until he was now standing behind me. "I think we can give him his privacy." I was getting a small peek at the man underneath everything else. He was hurt beyond words and that was the cause for his lack of faith.

"I can see that this is weighing heavily on your shoulders, doctor. What will it hurt if I were just to talk to a couple of the locals on your behalf? I don't even have to tell them that it is you was asking and I might be able to get better results. There is one such kid named Stefan that has his ear to the pulse of the island. If anybody can find your father, it would be him." He shrugged his shoulders like he didn't care anymore. He left me wondering if I should even help him but then it was my time to turn the other cheek.

"Bethany, I know that look and it appears that we're both going to get into the middle of this. Sometimes I wonder what people would do without us. Then again we were sent here for a reason from the great man himself. We can't shirk our duty. We need to keep helping people, even if they are reluctant to receive it." He might've been telling me to back away from the doctor, but his true intention was to keep us both from coming to blows. "Just do what you need to, Bethany. He doesn't need to know all the details."

I helped Jacob back to bed, still looking out of the corner of my eye towards the doctor. I was going to make a difference in his life, even if he didn't want me to. I was going to do this because it was the right thing to do. He needed to have closure. If that meant that I would bring him bad news, then he was just going to have to live with it. The devastation of the island was on a grand scale. Those that were killed were documented. There were records somewhere and if anybody could find them, it would be this kid.

I had seen him work his magic on a few people and I was quite amazed by the fact that he could get practically anything. Life on the island was a hardship for most, but he was one of those ones that were survivors. His entire family was killed in the quake, but he remained as resilient and strong as ever.

Chapter 5

Unfortunately, I couldn't find Stefan and apparently he had gone off the grid for the last couple of days. "I told you that I didn't want you to bother and now you tell me that you can't even help. Why would you try to get my hopes up and then dash them? I was starting to think that you might be the answer, but now I see that maybe you were just another problem." I didn't have to tell the doctor that I had tried to contact Stefan. I was trying to be honest.

"William, it doesn't matter, because he is not the only source of information. I can talk to the locals, send out feelers and see what comes of it."

"Bethany, I don't know why you're even considering this. I've been here for two years and the locals can be very unforgiving. They won't talk to me and I tried to be the *Gut* Samaritan and bring them whatever they need, but they only take and never give back. Being from a mixed marriage has been daunting enough, but now that my entire family has been ripped apart, I need my father even more. I'm not naïve to think that he survived the quake. I just want the opportunity to see if I can find him. I'm not saying that I wouldn't want a reunion, but at least I want a chance to say goodbye." I could understand that.

"I think the locals will be a little bit more forthcoming with us than with you. No offense, but you really are hard to approach in the best of circumstances. I can only imagine what you're like when you try to browbeat information out of somebody. Your approach might not be seen as goodwill. It might be that you're coming off as caustic and bitter. Nobody wants to be around somebody like that."

"I'm still hesitant to let you reach out to the locals. They only seem to stay in one select circle. They never let anybody into that circle, so why you think that you can is beyond me. I guess I have nothing to lose." That was high praise indeed. He all but told me that I could do whatever I wanted. He wasn't expecting results and he wasn't getting his hopes up.

Jacob had been here a day and he was going stir crazy. I could see him already getting dressed. He wasn't taking no for an answer. The doctor tried to stop him, but he was waved away in a dismissive nature. "Bethany, I hate to ask, but can you come over here and give me a hand with this?" I was more than happy to help him get onto his feet. I dressed him gingerly, trying to avoid those injuries as much as possible. He was already bandaged on both arms and you could see the discomfort in his eyes.

"I'm not sure it's a good idea for you to be walking around so early. I know the doctor would rather keep you here for another day. I know how stubborn you can be. Jacob, I just want you to promise me that you will take it easy. Do light duties and not anything strenuous. If you can promise that, then I would be glad to help you get dressed the rest of the way." I helped him into his white shirt. He lifted his legs one at a time and put them into the black trousers.

"I can't promise that I'm not going to work, Bethany. It's in my blood and these people need me. What I can do is try and not over exert myself. If I get tired, I will stop and rest. That's the best that I can offer you." It would have to be good enough, but it didn't mean that I had to like it. Even as he was walking, I could see that he was about to buckle underneath the strain.

I was about to reach out to him, but he was already going through the flap in the tent and back out to the outside. I stood there and watched. He looked towards the sun, closed eyes and lifted his head with the air slapping him in the face. I followed behind, my long plaid skirt hanging just above my ankles. I had to hold onto my bonnet. The wind was fierce, but it was mostly gusts that only lasted a couple of seconds and then diminished.

"Despite his misgivings, I'm still going to try to help him." He smiled, knowing full well that I would never back down or surrender. "He needs us and even he doesn't think so, he does. Maybe, if we do this for him, he will lighten up and find his way back to *Gott*."

"Bethany, you have the heart of a lion, but sometimes I think that we should both keep our distance. I've never been one to force anybody to swallow anything. I don't want to force our beliefs on anybody and that includes the doctor." It wouldn't hurt just to ask around. I've seen recently that the kids especially were more welcoming. The adults were struggling for life every day. They didn't have time to be pleasant and that was something that I could accept.

The kids had seen us as angels of mercy and it was those connections that I was going to use to try to find Williams' father. I found out that his name was Reginald. He didn't have a last name. Apparently, his mother had told him that one bit of information on her deathbed. It wasn't very much to go with, but it would have to suffice.

Chapter 6

"Bethany, are you sure that we shouldn't have something for a bribe? Maybe some chocolate or some kind of toy to loosen those lips?" I didn't want to be that kind of person. If I couldn't get the information by my goodwill and nature, then why bother.

"I think that we've shown these people that we can be trusted. They see us every day trying to help them the best we can. If that's not enough to garner some goodwill, then I don't know what is. Jacob, I think we both know that the locals will talk to us. It's time that we put that to *gut* use." We had been walking for a couple of hours, knowing full well that we were going to come to a village that was nearby.

Kids were running around playing with soccer balls that were given to them by the humanitarian aid workers. It was something to give them a semblance of hope for better days to come.

"Excuse me, but I would like to talk to all of you. I was addressing the crowd of six that were now stunned into silence by our presence. "I think you all know who we are. We've been very fortunate to be here for you. I have to say that we love your country. It's too bad that this happened to you, but we are going to do our best to make it right." They were staring at each other. I wasn't sure if they were going to be easy to talk to. One of them appeared ready to talk for the rest of them.

"We know who you are and we appreciate everything that you've done for us. We all know that you didn't come here just for that." He was very intuitive and his eyes were alive, almost like he had been forced to become an adult too early in life. "I'm guessing that you want information." Again, he was putting words into my mouth, but I couldn't deny the fact that we were there for some kind of assistance.

"I would like to ask you to find somebody for us. I know that it's not going to be easy, but it's something that can't be avoided. There is a man named Reginald. I do have a photo, but it's very old." They gathered around and peered over each other shoulders to take a look at it. "I would like you to talk to your parents, Elders or anybody else that you can get your hands on. Between all six of you, I'm sure that there is an answer out there somewhere." They smiled, but I thought that they were going to turn tail and leave me with nothing but egg on my face.

"On behalf of my friends, we accept this challenge. Normally, we would be asking you for a favor in return, but you have done more than enough already. Trust me, things could be worse." For this kid to say that, meant that he had hope in his heart and enough love to weather any kind of storm. "I think I know where you can find the answers that you seek." With that, he had turned and began walking, carrying a stick and using it to push his way through the underbrush.

We both looked at each other and instantly knew that we were going to have to follow him. It took a bit of doing, but we finally reached another village no more than ½ hour's walk from the last one. This one looked like it had seen better days.

The kid stopped at this small encampment and then he pointed towards a small enclosure. It looked like it was going to fall down at any second. The roof was sagging and it appeared to be on its last legs. "This kid's grandmother has a son named Reginald. Most people call him Reggie. Come to think of it, we haven't seen him since the earthquake." That was all that needed to be said and he turned and walked away like he wasn't supposed to be here.

The door opened and standing there with a dirty face and clothing covered in what look like mud was this child of about eight years old. "Come in already." In wasn't even sure if it was safe to enter onto the premises. I looked towards Jacob and before I even said a word, he was already nodding his head an agreement. I guess our Amish background made us want to help.

"I'm way ahead of you, Bethany." He went outside and I heard him on the roof within minutes. He was fixing what needed to be fixed.

I saw that the kid was out of water. I looked around for any source of H2O, but unfortunately there was none to be found.

"I'm sorry, but I don't have anything to offer you. We have some stale bread and water is about an hour's walk west of here." I almost wanted to cry. Instead I picked up the huge water jug and began lugging it into a nearby field. It was well marked with footprints and it took me awhile to get down to the stream. I filled the jug to capacity, put it on my shoulder and began to lug it back.

When I got within distance, I saw Jacob still on the roof. He had secured it by replacing old boards with ones that were lying around down below. Somebody had dropped off some wood, but didn't get a chance to complete the task.

It was getting dark and seeing that we wanted to meet his grandmother, we decided to stay and lend a hand to the village. We'd already finished for the day volunteering and now we were doing the same thing in a different capacity. We helped them tend to their gardens, worked to keep a roof over their heads and even went back to the water source at least five times. I think we both knew that we were only two people and that we could only do so much.

By the time that the sun was going down, we were exhausted and couldn't even keep our eyes open. I put my hand over Jacob's chest, feeling his heart beating underneath my fingertips. It soothed me in a way that made it possible for me to slip into a deep slumber.

Chapter 7

"What the hell is going on in here? Both Jacob and I jumped to our feet, half asleep and feeling a little embarrassed. We had slept on the floor, while the kid was sleeping in the next room. This woman looked like she could be a force to be reckoned with. "Somebody better tell me what the hell is going on here, or I'm going to get my pitchfork."

"Grandma, please don't do anything to these people. They came here for an answer about Reginald. They didn't have to stay, but they did. They fixed the roof and brought water to me and the other villagers. They are *gut* people and they deserve your respect." The kid was something else. The grandmother looked at him, smiled and then ruffled the boy's hair.

"If what he is saying is true, then by all means stay as long as you want. As for Reginald, I'm afraid that I have some bad news." I didn't like where this was going, but we had come too far to stick our heads in the sand. "I was just informed a few days ago that they found a body that matched the description I had given them when the earthquake happened. I was hoping that they were wrong, but I have just come back from identifying the body. It is Reginald. I'm afraid that you've come a long way for nothing. The only thing I can give you is my condolences. He was a fine boy, a fine son and somebody that everybody looked up to."

We found out that her name was Sonya. She regaled us with stories of Reginald's youth. We actually found ourselves laughing at his exploits. The only thing that wasn't laughable was that we were going to have to come back to William with empty hands. At least he would know that his father was gone. It might give him that closure that he was looking for.

"I'm sorry that I wasn't able to give you better news." She hadn't even asked why we wanted to know. She was just very calm, even though she was probably grieving deeply inside. I could feel her pain. I think she was trying to keep up a front for the child. She must have brought him in when the earthquake happened. That showed just what kind of person she was. She would give the shirt off her back to anybody that needed it. "Please, don't be a stranger. I can see that you mean well, but our village is not your problem. Come visit sometime when we're back on our feet."

We left there feeling like the wind was knocked out of us. "Bethany, you know that he's not going to take this very well. Why don't you let me talk to him and maybe

I can help him see that the future isn't as bleak as he thinks it is. He's still alive and that means he can still make a true difference." It didn't look like he was going to be easy to talk to. If Jacob thought that he could lessen the blow, then I thought why not give him a chance.

"Jacob, try and make him see that it's not the end of the world." It was going to be hard for us to do that, considering that the Dr. was a bit pigheaded. "We may not be able to bring his father back, but maybe we can give him something else to hold onto. You can tell him about Sonya and that might give him a reason to go and talk to her. That would enable him to find out about his father in a way that he had never had before." It was hot outside and the sun was beating down on us. Thankfully, we had hats to keep us from getting sunstroke.

We had to get back, because we still had a lot of *schaffe* to do before the new arrivals were due to come any day. I don't know what our next destination was, but I could only assume that we weren't going home yet.

I had been in touch with my daughter Rebekah. She was very happy to hear from me and I even sent her letters detailing my *schaffe*. I wanted her to know that my absence was for a reason. She was amazing and I didn't see any resentment or hear anything from her voice when I had her on the phone. I had to give my mother in law credit for trekking all the way to find a phone. We didn't have a whole of time to talk, but it was enough to keep me from worrying about her. I would always think about her, but at least now I knew that she was in good hands.

"I know that you're thinking about Rebekah." How he knew that was beyond me "It's written all over your face. Besides, who else would you be thinking about at a time like this? That family has seen its fair share of loss. It must bring back a lot of bad memories for you."

"I don't know if I even have any bad memories anymore. I've gotten past the loss by remembering the *gut* times and having you by my side. I would say that you gave me a new lease on life, Jacob and that is something that I can never repay."

"Bethany, you don't need to repay anything. You've done the same thing for me." We made our way back and by the time we reached the tent it was well after 9:00 AM.

We hesitated for a second outside the tent. We finally steeled our resolve and went in. We didn't even have to say anything to William, who saw the answer from the expression on our face. "I was afraid of that, but you just confirmed my suspicions."

Jacob tried to go to him, but he was rejected. I could see the devastation in the doctor's eyes and Jacob was doing all he could to let him know that he wasn't alone. "I think that you should go see Sonya."

"Young man that is the last thing that I'm going to do. It will only bring up the loss of my father. Nothing *gut* can come from that." Jacob was out of his element and this man was not one to easily listen to reason "I need to get back to work. It's the one thing that I know that I can do better than anybody else." His ego was huge, but maybe he needed that time to calm down in an environment that he knew better than he knew himself. Either way, the loss of his father had hit him hard and there was nothing that Jacob could do to lessen the blow.

Chapter 8

We needed him to have the time to grieve in private. We left him alone and went back to our jobs. He might have been out of sight, but he was never once out of our thoughts.

It was about 2:00 PM, when I finally ventured to look in on him. There was nobody in the medical tent and he was now standing there with a bottle of liquor. It was sitting right in front of him and he was holding onto the bottle like it was his own personal life line. If that wasn't bad enough, he was also holding a needle in his hands. He took a swig of the liquor, and then plunged the needle into his arm.

I could see what it was from my vantage point. It was morphine and he was mixing that with alcohol, so they could deal with his grief. I didn't know if it was my place to say anything to him. Perhaps, I could reach out to somebody that would be able to have a more lasting impact.

"I hope that you are watching me from heaven mother and father. You left me with nothing but my *schaffe*. No family to speak of. I don't know what I'm going to do without the two of you in my life. I was hoping that I would find answers here in Haiti, but these two years have been for nothing. I thought that if I helped all of these people that *Gott* might have mercy on me. He was devastated. He took another swig from the bottle. He was using it to dull the pain as much as possible. If that wasn't going to do the trick, then the morphine that was swimming upstream in his veins was going to be keeping him feeling no pain whatsoever.

I wanted to reach out to him, but I turned around and went back to see the Bishop. He saw me coming and he must have known something was wrong, because he stretched out his hands and welcomed me into his warm embrace.

"I don't know what's the matter, child, but whatever it is I'm sure that we can deal with it together. I've known you for a long time, Bethany and you're one of the most compassionate people that I have ever met." I just couldn't voice what I wanted to say. All of a sudden it came out of my mouth like a wave came over me. He listened intently to what I had to say. "I know this must have been hard for you to come to me like this. I appreciate that you gave me that trust. I think that I can help this man. Leave it with me." I knew that if anybody could get him the help that he deserved, it would be the Bishop.

I felt infinitely better. That was short lived when I saw a confrontation between the Bishop and William. They weren't alone and Father Jensen was right along for the ride. There were two others, but I had no idea who they were. "I'm sorry, William, but this is the only way that it's going to work. If you don't agree to get help, then your job is done." I couldn't believe what I was seeing. He was being confronted at the lowest point in his life.

"I don't need your help and I quit." He walked away and disappeared within the labyrinth of tents.

The Bishop came over to me "I'm sorry, but I had to do what was right for everybody. We can't have the doctor prescribing morphine for himself. He has to get his demons under control. The only way to do that is to take a leave and come back fresh and ready to go at it again. The decision is made. If he decides to leave, then he is going to do himself an injustice. He needs to see that we are just trying to help." If I'd known that he was going to lose his job, I'm not sure that I would've gone to seek the counsel of the Bishop.

"I didn't want any of this. I thought that you would just have a talk with him."

"Bethany, you have to see it from our point of view. If we allowed him to continue to practice medicine, then somebody might be injured by his abuse of his own

body. We can't have that. I know you understand that."
I did, but right now my rage was fueling the way that I
was voicing my concern.

"I shouldn't have come to you at all." I felt like I had
just given the doctor a reason to draw ever deeper into
the bottle and drugs. There had to be a way to fix this. I
had done considerable damage on my own.

Jacob came over and hugged me from behind "You did
what you thought you should and you shouldn't feel
any guilt for that, Bethany. Trust that everything will
work out the way that it's supposed to. We just need to
find a way to give the doctor a reason to stay or at least
go to rehab." He was saying everything that I needed to
hear. I was stricken with this moment of intense hatred.
I didn't hate the Bishop for what he had done, because
he was only looking out for everybody concerned. The
person I hated was myself for allowing this to get this
far.

Instead of leaving the poor man alone, I had interfered
in his business once again. He had lost his livelihood,
his only form of revenue and it was all due to me
sticking my nose where it didn't belong. I thought that
if anybody could help it would be the Bishop. He didn't
even try and his way of helping was to tell the Board of
Directors that their Dr. was self-medicating. It wasn't

right. I wanted him to get some kind of guidance from the Lord's words. Instead they had given him an ultimatum that made him lash out in an unforeseen way. Without him around, people would suffer, because getting another Dr. into this region wasn't going to be easy.

I did find out that for the interim a Dr. from a nearby district would be splitting his duties from this region to the other. It was going to have to be good enough. I heard through the Grapevine that the Dr. was going to be leaving on a plane later in the afternoon.

Chapter 9

"I know that you mean well, Bethany but this has to be our decision. He can't work here if he's going to be doing something like that." I had reached out to the Board of Directors and was now sitting in front of them with my hat in my hand. Not literally, but figuratively speaking anyway. "We do appreciate your concern for his wellbeing, but this is something that he is going to have to go through."

"I implore you to give him another chance. He's a *gut* Dr. He just lost his way. We need to give him a reason to pick himself back up from the devastation and loss of his own mother and father. We've all going through similar things in our lives. I'm sure that all you wanted to do was hide in a hole and die. I know that he can't come back the way he is. Would you be amenable to him getting his job back if he were to go to rehab to get clean?" They'd already said that that was what he needed to do, but I had yet to hear that they were going to welcome him back with open arms.

"Bethany, I know that you came to me hoping that I would have all the answers. Sometimes those answers are not something that you want to hear." The board of directors were shaking their head unanimously. They were all in agreement.

"I don't care about any of that, Bishop. What I do care about is William and what he's going to do next. I need an answer to what I just asked. Would you welcome him back if he were to go to rehab as suggested?"

There were hushed whispers around the table and they were huddled together in a secretive way. When they separated, they allowed the Bishop to speak for the lot of them. Jacob was standing by my side holding my hand, giving me the courage that I needed to confront these individuals.

"I've talked to the board and they agree that he is a talent that shouldn't be wasted. They have agreed that he can come back if and only when he gets clean. There is a two month course in the States and we want him to commit himself for the duration of that stay. He has to follow all the rules, never waver from the treatment and then he can walk out of there with his head held high." It was something, but now we had to find a way to give him a reason to do it.

As we walked out of there, I said to Jacob "I think we need to go back to Sonya. I don't know why, but I feel like she was being less than honest. There is something that she's keeping from us."

"I never got anything like that from her, but I'm not stupid enough to tell you that I would go against your womanly instincts." He was right to do so, because that would only anger me further. "If we need to go see Sonya, then we go and see Sonya." This time, we were able to borrow a couple of bicycles. This made the journey twice as fast and for the first time in a long time we were relating to our youth in a different way.

When we arrived at the village, we saw the child that we had spoken to outside chopping wood. The grandmother was sitting there and doing some sort of crochet. She rose up wearing what can only be described as a long unflattering dress of multi colors. "I'm glad that you could come back, but what brings you back in such a hurry?" We told her everything that was going on and she began to think so hard that I thought that the top of her head was going to explode.

"We don't know what to do to prove to him that life is worth living. He has lost all his family and now he wants nothing to do with anybody." I was pleading to her for something.

"I wasn't going to tell you this, but he hasn't lost all of his family." It was then that I found eyes drawing ever closer to the young kid sweating to pick up the axe in both of his hands. "Samuel is not just a kid that I have brought into my home. He is my grandson and is Williams's half-brother." She showed us documentation, birth certificate and blood work that proved beyond a shadow of a doubt that Samuel was indeed William's half-brother. "I'm not going to stop him from leaving, but I can't take the journey with him. If Samuel wants to go, then he has my blessing."

Sonya was not in the greatest of health, but she was a strong person. We all sat down with Samuel and told him the unbiased truth. He looked at us with concern, but then his little eyes lit up at the prospect of having a sibling.

"I don't want to leave my grandmother, but I also want to help my brother." We didn't get into the details. We told him that William was hurting and needed somebody to come to his rescue "I want to do the right thing and I think that I would like to get to know him." Out of the mouths of babes.

Chapter 10

We didn't have a moment to lose. We waited until the Samuel was able to gather up all of the little belongings he had. He even had a passport, which was given to him as a gift one year from his father Reginald. He wanted him to travel the world. I think he was secretly hoping that they could do that together. Now that he was gone, Samuel was alone, but now he didn't have to be.

Sonya told us when he was gone that she didn't have all that long to live. She wasn't going to be around to see Samuel grow up and she was just grateful that he would have William to hold onto. She made us promise not to tell William or Samuel any of this. She wanted them to live their life and knowing that they were out there and together was enough for her.

"That is one strong lady." I couldn't have said it better myself. Jacob was not exactly happy with the situation.

"I know that our instinct is telling us to tell them everything, but it's not our secret to tell. Jacob, we've gone down this road a couple of times already and maybe we should learn from our mistakes." He was solemnly nodding his head and I knew that we would keep her secret and never tell anybody.

Samuel was giddy with anticipation. He was bouncing up and down like he was on a sugar high. We then took our leave of Sonya. Before we left, he hugged her goodbye, holding onto her with everything that his little hands could muster. Finally, he relinquished his hold and we went to the Airport.

It didn't take us long to get there. Thankfully we had the Bishop standing by just in case. He was able to procure the bus that we had been brought in with. He was waiting for us at the edge of the village, the motor running and his foot firmly planted on the gas. There was only a dust cloud behind us. We moved around each individual pothole, making sure that we weren't going to wreck the vehicle before we got to our final destination.

"I think what the two of you are doing here is admirable, but are you sure that William is the right person to raise this child?" I had thought about myself. I could only hope that having Samuel in his life would give him a reason to stand up on his own two feet.

"I don't know what I'm doing. I'm just doing what I think is right." That was all that was needed to be said and we finally arrived at the Airport. The tarmac had an airplane ready to take off. They were refueling and it wouldn't be long before they were airborne.

The kid was hanging to me and Jacob. Our two hands were clasped into his little ones and making our way down the hallway. "I'm sorry, but you can't go any further than here." Security was tight, but we had to get in there. "If this was some kind of emergency, maybe we would be able to make some sort of exception."

This was my chance to pull at her heart strings. "This as a matter of family and two brothers that didn't even know that the other existed needs to be united. One brother is falling from grace, while the other one is ready to lift him up into the light. Let us go through with your security guards presence. That way you'll know that we are no threat to you or the staff." I felt like I was swimming upstream and that the only current that was in my way was this diminutive little woman behind the counter.

"I don't normally do this, but your story made a tear come to my eye." It must've been metaphorical, because I didn't see any sort of tear. It didn't stop her from allowing us to enter and there standing and getting ready to board the plane was William.

"You can't go." He turned at the sound of our voice. Jacob and I had said the same thing at exactly the same time.

"I think that the both of you should leave me alone. Don't you think you've done enough already?" He was angry, but I was gonna have to defuse the situation and make him see his brother.

"I know that you're upset with me, but I think I have somebody here that would like to meet you." Jacob and I separated and there standing between us was this young African American kid named Samuel.

"My name is Samuel and my father was Reginald. That makes us brothers." The realization that he had family made him drop to his knees in front of the kid. "I want you to know that you're not alone. We are now together." He looked at us trying to find an answer, but the kid was saying everything that needed to be said. "I want to go with you. I have my passport and I'm ready to leave anytime. They tell me that you're hurting. I want to help you." The doctor rose to his feet and looked down at this small smiling child and began to smile himself.

"I don't know what I can do to thank you for this." He didn't need to do anything, except of course to buy the kid a ticket, which he did readily. He promised us that he would go into rehab. During that Samuel would stay with a friend that he trusted with his life. When he got out, he would collect him and they would both come back here to work side by side. This was the best of both worlds and maybe they would both have a chance to comfort their grandmother in her hour of need. It would be nice to see this family come together, at least until Sonya was able to reunite with those that had already passed on.

BOOK 4 – Groundbreaking

Rachel H. Kester

Chapter 1

I was getting a little tired of the constant delays and to be honest, I was finding myself homesick. It wasn't like I didn't deserve a little time with my child. I was working very hard every single day to help these people stand on their own two feet. I enjoyed putting my hand on a hammer, striking against the wood and watching as the structure began to form into something that was livable. I was the only woman that was doing this type of job. I don't think that they were enjoying the fact that I was taking on the role of a man.

"Bethany, you've shown some amazing aptitude and I wouldn't think that somebody could get so good at carpentry in such a short period of time. I'm not going to say that it's only because I'm a good teacher. It takes a good student to become the sponge that is necessary to learn. You might be my wife and it might be my place to keep you safe, but I know that you a stubborn and are going to do whatever you want anyway."

Jacob was my husband. He liked to think that he was the man of the family and that he was the one that wore the pants. He was finding out in a hurry that I was independent, had a mind of my own and had gotten that way because of the fact that my former husband had died quite unexpectedly. I had to take on the role of not only mother but father as well. I was working in the field and keeping a roof over our head by making things with my bare hands. I actually got a lot of pride from those that told me that I had made the best stuff.

"Jacob, it's nice to know that I am not relegated to passing out water or food. I was actually seeing my work come to fruition." We had also been counseling others in the area. We were going from town to town on those off days that we weren't building. It was there that we found those that were struggling to make sense of it all. We counseled them with the help of the Bible. That was where we got answers ourselves when we were feeling like life didn't make any sense. "I know that they say that we were supposed to go home last week, but so far the other volunteers haven't arrived."

"Bethany, I heard from the Deacon and he says that their passports had to be updated. It's going to take time. I know that you're missing Rebekah. I sometimes think that it might've been a good idea to bring her with us. Then I look around and I really don't want her to be a part of this. To remain innocence and childlike is a gift that we can give her and I don't intend to take that away from her anytime soon." I felt the same way. It didn't mean that I didn't feel the tugging on my heart each and every day. I knew that she was in good hands and that our families would take more than good care of her.

"I'm glad you said that, because I was wondering the same thing. I know that she's better off where she's at. There comes a time when a mother needs the comforting arms of her child. I'm getting to that point and to be honest, I'm starting to feel like this will never end" I knew that this life was not for everybody and that those that had ventured into humanitarian aid work were a different breed of people. I had to put myself in the shoes of those that we were helping. I was looking around and seeing the devastation on everybody's faces.

The only thing that was keeping me going was the fact that I could look at my daughter in my mind's eye. I can remember her as clear as day, the way that she smiled and tugged on my sleeve outside when I was chopping wood. I saw the young woman underneath it all and knew that she was going to be one real heartbreaker. I pitied the first guy that tried to put her in her place. They would find out that her mother had taught her to be strong and resilient.

"Bethany, just keep thinking about her. I'm sure that we'll be leaving here as soon as possible. I think that we are just about finished with what we have to do on this house. We're going to have to turn it over to those that are more proficient in electrical and plumbing work. That leaves us time to go and put on a counseling session by the water. I've already heard from a few people that are going to attend. Apparently there is somebody new that has just come on the scene." I had no idea who he might be talking about, but if they need our help, then I was obligated to at least give them the benefit of my experience.

Jacob had taken off his hat to wipe his brow. It was letting me see his beautiful eyes and the way that they looked at me with love and compassion. I never did think that I would get over my husband. To be honest there would always be a spot for him in my heart. When Jacob came along, I started to see that there was room for another. He had shown me that love could take many forms. I did love him, but not in the same way that I did my deceased husband. It was different, pure and so new that it made my heart leap for joy every time that I woke up beside Jacob.

We were making our way back, me holding onto my skirt, which was a little unusual when you put into context that I was working with my hands. I actually had calluses, something that I was getting used to and then we heard a voice that was raised.

"I don't care what you say, Deacon Alba. I want to see my wife and not even God himself is going to stand in my way. She has my daughter and I've come here personally to collect the both of them and take them back to where they belong. I can't believe that she had the gall to leave me in the middle of the night. There was no note or anything, leaving me to track her down through the parish. I won't be treated like this and I'll be damned if I allow a woman to stand up to me." We couldn't see who was talking. He was obviously distraught and his anger was seeping through the cracks in the exterior.

"Lucas, I think that you should calm down and think about what you're going to do when you finally see the both of them. I know what you did and I'm not here to judge, only to help. Lucas, you know that she came here to get away from you. The fact that you came a thousand miles to see her only tells me that you do love her in your own way. You just have to get your emotions in check, or you're just going to make things worse." We turned the corner and saw this man gripping the lapels of Deacon Alba's shirt.

"I don't have to do anything and it's my right as her husband to take care of her in my own way. I don't know what she has been telling you, but I've only put my hands on her because she just doesn't listen. I've apologized over and over again and I don't know what else she expects from me." The anger was superseding his good judgment and I could see that he was going to strike the Deacon any minute.

His fist was raised. Jacob was right there to hold him back. That fist slammed into the hand of Jacob. Jacob was standing strong and looking this man in the eye. He was not budging an inch. "I think that you of all people can get something from our counseling session. Why don't you join us? In fact, my wife and I have thought about using another form of therapy and you might just be the one that we can make a test subject." I knew that he was talking about carpentry. We had often thought that having people that were hurting work with their hands might give them an outlet that they needed to stop and listen to their own heart.

Chapter 2

I don't know how Jacob convinced him, but finally Lucas relented and came with us to the water's edge to hear what everybody else was talking about. He didn't say anything. He was listening to each and every one of these people talk about their loss and how it had affected their lives.

"My mother was pinned underneath some rubble and I could see that her legs were crushed and that blood was coming out of her mouth. I knew that she was going to die and I think that she knew it as well. I don't know what gave her strength, but she tried to comfort me, instead of thinking about what she was going through. Her strength was amazing and I will miss her until the day I die and am reunited with her. I see her everywhere in the way that the trees are blowing around us, the flowers blooming in the hills and I know that she is looking down from above." Able was a young man of 17 years old, who had to grow up a little too quickly. He was now taking care of his two siblings, while helping them grow up to be the men that they were going to become.

"Able, I think that your mother is here. You can see in the words of the Bible that God has now taken her in as one of his emissaries. She is standing by his side in the Glory of heaven. All you have to do is look at the stars and know that she's there." I could see a lone tear in his eyes. I felt the same kind of pain that he felt when my husband left me so abruptly. "I know how you're feeling and I have been down that road myself. It's not pleasant, but it's a part of life and is something that we're going to have to live with."

"My wife is right and you know that you can all come and talk to us any time that you need to vent. We know the signs. At first you are reluctant to believe that it has actually happened, then you move on to bargaining and then you finally accept that they're gone. It's a long and arduous journey and not one that you should take lightly. You can't skip a step. If you do, you're only hurting yourself and the ones around you." Jacob and I were both watching Lucas very carefully. He had softened a little bit after hearing Able's story.

"I know that we've been talking to all of you for some time. I know that it takes more than just lip service to find the answers that you're looking for. We would like to invite all of you to come to our work site tomorrow morning at the crack of dawn. We're going to put a hammer into your hands and you're going to work through your issues by pounding your frustration out of a nail. I want you to use that as an outlet. It will help you to let go of those hurt feelings. We wouldn't even suggest this, but I have found that it is therapeutic and I would like to share that with those that would like to try it themselves." I was sitting in a Lotus position, my skirt fanned out around my legs and everybody else was sitting on their knees listening to everything that we had to say.

I saw that everybody was in agreement. They were more than happy to take part in this therapeutic work program. "I don't see how pounding a nail into a piece of wood is going to do me any good." Everybody turned at the caustic and acid tone in Lucas' voice. "I don't need help. What I need is my family. Why you insist on blocking me is beyond me. If I want to, I could just go there myself, but I have promised the Deacon that I would at least give this a try. I don't think it's going to do any good, but I don't see any harm in it." His voice might've been laced with sarcasm and anger, but underneath it all, I could see that Able's words had really struck a chord.

"I don't suppose that you have something to say about a certain loss of your own, Lucas?" I knew that his animosity and his anger were coming from somewhere. I wasn't quite sure how to go about revealing that particular demon. "Everybody here is not going to judge you and whatever you say stays in the confines of this group." I could see that he was contemplating what he wanted to say. At the last second, he got up and walked away with his boots stomping into the ground. It was a work in progress and we were just going to have to be patient. Hopefully he would open up on his own.

I was about to go after him, but Jacob put his hand on my shoulder and looked at me sternly "I don't think it's our place to force our beliefs on him. We can take solace in the fact that he is at least listening to reason. We need to give him space. It's the only way that he is going to finally see past the hatred and rage. We both know that it's not of his doing. It comes from something in his past. Until he finally admits his problem, the only thing we can do is be there for him." I knew that Jacob was telling the truth, but it didn't make anything easier.

"Is he going to be OK?" This was Able, someone that had come to us with his heart broken into a million pieces. I was seeing those pieces slowly being put back together again. He might've still had that loss to deal with, but at least he had people that he could talk to that would understand. "I know where he's coming from. I've been there myself. It's not easy to let others in. It makes you feel like you are weak and can't take care of yourself." I understood all of that, but it didn't help matters any. I still felt like I should go to him and get him to unburden his soul.

"I know that you want to help, Able, but all we can do is wait and see if our words get through to him. Right now, he is only concerned by the fact that his family left him. He feels betrayed. He's taking them leaving as a personal attack against him. He needs to realize that time is the answer. He might see that his wife and child had being taken away from him for a reason. He needs to see that it's not all about him and that they have feelings as well. He can't constantly use his fists to get his point across." I'd talked to Deacon Alba and I had found out the story behind Lucas being here.

He was a bit abusive with his wife. After the last time that she got a bruise on her arm, she had decided to get their child out of line of fire before something happened. Her church was involved in the humanitarian aid work. It was decided that she would get some distance in Haiti. Unfortunately, Lucas didn't take this kindly and decided to track them down by any means necessary. I was kind of looking forward to what would happen when he got his hands on a hammer. For me it gave me a way to express my anger towards my late husband's death.

Chapter 3

As I was standing by the water's edge, thinking about him, Jacob put his hand into mine. "I know what you're thinking. I would never presume to tell you that you can't think about him. He was after all a big part of your life and without him there would be no us. He had to pass on before we could get together. I wish that I had gotten to know him, but I think that I have a pretty good idea of what kind of man he is by what I see in you." It was nice of him to say that and it gave me comfort to know that he didn't feel jealous about my thoughts for my former husband.

"I will always think about him, because we share a bond with my daughter Rebekah. I think that children are our future. If Lucas could see through his red hot rage, he might be able to finally see that he has nothing without them." I put my head on his shoulder. We just sat there and watched the water lapping against the bank in front of us. We could see that we were just cogs in the machinery. That everybody played their part, regardless if it was a small or the more significant one.

It was then that I heard a vehicle start up and what sounded like some kind of commotion. We arrived just in time to see that Lucas was in a fistfight with a couple of young men of African descent. He had wailed on them with his fist, grabbed onto their keys and was now making his way over to one of the grey jeeps. He had the key in the door. Jacob walked over to him and stopped him before he did anything that he would regret.

Jacob had grabbed his key and pulled it away from his grasp. He didn't even have a chance to think about what he was going to do next. "Give me that back. You don't want to get in the middle of this, Jacob. This is about family." I felt the raw nerve from way over here. It was strained to the point that he just needed to lash out at something. That was the reason why I had decided to put this program into play.

"I'm not going to let you do this, Lucas. You don't know what you're doing. It's only going to make matters worse. You need time to get this anger under control."

"I don't need to do anything. So get out of my way or I'm going to flatten you." Jacob wasn't moving, standing strong with his muscular physique ready to take any blow that was coming his way. "I'm warning you. Believe me; you don't want to test me." Again, Jacob wasn't moving.

"Lucas, this is not the way." Just as he finished his comment, Lucas tried to strike out with his fist. It was clumsy. Jacob was able to duck away from it in time. He didn't try to strike back. "You don't want to do this. This is not the time for something like this. You need to take this and read it tonight. Let the words take you on a journey of self-discovery." Jacob had placed the Bible in his hand. He looked at it like it was a foreign entity.

"Jacob, I don't see how this is going to help me any." He had no idea what kind of power he had in his hands. With one single solitary word from those pages, he might see that who he had really been lashing out at was himself.

I could see that the two men that he had knocked to the ground were now getting up. They were dusting themselves off and looking towards Lucas for some kind of retaliation. I defused the situation by going over to them and explaining that he was not acting like himself. "Just give him time to heal. He didn't mean anything by it and I would appreciate it as a gesture of good faith that you just turn the other cheek." They were both very accommodating and not one had decided to see what they could do for some kind of revenge. "I appreciate your understanding at this time. Please, don't be afraid to come to me with your concerns about this or anything else." They were nodding their head and then they walked away with one more glance towards Lucas.

I came back over and saw that Lucas was now holding onto that Bible for dear life. "I don't know what this is going to help, but I will try. That's the only thing that I can promise." He walked away, the Bible very much a part of him. I can only hope that he was a man of his word and that he would read several of those phrases. I had even marked a few well-chosen verses that might strike home.

"I don't know how I was able to keep myself from hitting him back, Bethany."

"I think it's because that you are a good man, Jacob. You know that he's hurting and that you don't want to make anything more of it. He needs our understanding and patience." He was looking at me, kissing my hand on the back of it and then putting his hand around my shoulders.

"I really do think that you are a good influence on these people, Bethany." I could say the same thing for him, but I don't think that I had to. We were both very instrumental in not only rebuilding the society, but also rebuilding their faith. I still missed Rebekah. I could take some comfort in the fact that we were helping those that couldn't help themselves.

"Jacob, if we can help those that we counsel every day, then I don't see any reason why we can't help Lucas. He's just lost and needs somebody to guide him into the light. I think we have taken the first step by giving him the Bible. It is after all his words that will make him see his true path." God was looking after all of us in his own way. Even if we don't see the answer to our prayers, doesn't mean that he wasn't listening.

Chapter 4

In the morning, it was time to put the new initiative into effect. I wasn't sure how it was going to be received. There was really only one way to find out. We were getting together with all those that had been counseled in the past. They were waiting for us, looking at their shoes and not quite knowing what they were going to do. Even Lucas had arrived on time. I thought that was never going to happen. He looked well rested and he was still holding onto that Bible like it was his own personal lifeline.

"Lucas, it's nice to see that you're here as well. I see that you have the Bible and I'm hoping that you did find some kind of comfort from the words." I watched as he looked at it and then back at me, before stepping up and getting into my own personal space.

"I know that you and Jacob mean well, but I feel sometimes that you are crowding me. Yes, I did read those verses in the bible and amazingly I did feel better. I don't know what I'm doing here. I've never picked up a hammer in my life. It's not something that a lawyer of my caliber would be found doing." That was essentially the reason why we had put this program together. "I really don't know what you think is going to happen." I knew that the possibility of resistance was going to be prevalent, but I was willing to take that risk.

"I see that everybody is here. Why don't we get started." Jacob had several hammers on hand and he was now passing them out like they were a gift from God. "I don't want you to do anything until I show you the basics. I'm sorry, I may have misspoken and what I meant by that is until we both show you the basics." I was glad that he caught himself. He was starting to sound a little chauvinistic. That was not the man that I had married.

Everybody was not sure of themselves and it took a lot of coaxing to get them to finally get a hang of it. I heard a lot of cursing, as many of those hammers were now striking the unforgiving surface of their thumb. I think after a while, people started to laugh at their own discomfort. Even Lucas was finding his rhythm.

"That's pretty good, but just keep your eye on the nail at all times, Lucas." He actually smiled at me, went back to what he was doing and not at all cursing my name. "Let me know if you need anything. I'll be over here helping the others."

"Bethany, before you go, I want to thank you for everything." I wasn't sure if I heard him right. "I mean

170

it and I know that I can be stubborn at times. It's something that I'm working on." I still wondered what the underlying reason for his anger was. It had to do with something from his childhood or maybe some kind of incident that had haunted him all of his life. "I don't know the reason why I'm like this. My father was a good man, but he was very strict. My parents died when I was no more than 12 years old. I guess I still have some residual anger over being abandoned. I didn't have any siblings and I was passed around from relative to relative, until I was old enough to care for myself." I was now getting a pretty clear picture of what his life was like. His father was domineering, but the worst of it all was that he was left alone so early in his childhood.

I went over to the others, constantly keeping vigil on Lucas to make sure that he wasn't just going to run off and go to the school house to get Laura and Jessica. They were his family. He thought that he had every right to see them. The fact that they didn't want to see him was a testament to what kind of man they thought he was. If they could see him now, they might feel differently.

At the end of the day, everybody was sweating but feeling like they had accomplished something. "I want you all to know that we both thank you for taking part in this therapy. We hope that it was every bit as helpful as it was for Bethany. She lost her husband and she deals with that every day. I know she finds the good book to help her through it. Manual labor also gives her a way to express herself without screaming or hiding something." Jacob was now standing there as majestic as ever. The sun was streaming down on him like he was an angel from heaven.

There was no denying that this therapy had made a lasting impact on each and every one of them. I could see even Lucas was affected. He was now looking at me and Jacob "I've never done this before, but it makes me feel like I'm a real man." I don't know if I would've put it quite like that. This was what he was getting out of it. "I feel like all of my anger has washed away. There is this weight on my shoulders that has been alleviated." I was glad that we could help him and along with the good book, I was sure that he could finally get his family back. "I now see that what I've done to my family is wrong. I owe them everything and I showed them by force instead of love."

Chapter 5

It was one thing to hear him say those words, but it was another thing to see if he was going to act accordingly. Jacob and I had come up with something that would show us that he was on his road to recovery.

"Watch where you're going." Jacob and I were both watching as this huge black man was now bumping into Lucas. It was by design, because we had put Tyrone up to playing his part. "I don't know what your problem is, but you owe me an apology." It was going to be interesting to see how he reacted. He had no idea that we were doing this.

"You were the one that bumped into me." At the very least, I could see that Lucas was not using his fists in anger. "I don't owe you a damn thing."

Tyrone pushed him, knocking him onto the ground and then stood over him menacingly. "I said that you owe me an apology. Didn't you hear me or do you have wax in your ears?" I could see Lucas balling up his fist. He was gritting his teeth like he was going to do something about this.

At the last second, he stopped, got back up onto his own two feet and stood his ground. "I apologize and please forgive me." It didn't sound sincere, but at least he was saying the words. "I wasn't watching where I was going."

Tyrone didn't push the issue, walking away like he had accepted his apology in the spirit that it was given. Lucas still looked like he was going to attack. Somehow he was able to reel in his emotions before they got the better of him.

I walked over holding onto my hat, making sure that the wind wasn't going to blow it off my head. "I saw what happened and I'm very proud of you." I felt like we were getting through to him and that he wasn't going to use violence as the answer for everything. "I thought for a minute that you were going to come to blows."

"I don't think I have to tell you how much I wanted to hit him. It took a lot of willpower not to make him eat my fist. I wanted to see his teeth come flying out of his head." I saw that he was struggling with that demon. At least he didn't give it power over him. It was a sure sign that he was now willing to at least talk about things. "This whole thing stems from my father and mother. I know that now and I have the both of you to thank for that. I'd been to therapy, but it never lasted more than a couple of sessions. I guess I really did need to vent my anger in a more constructive way." I didn't consider myself a professional by any means. I did know that I had the word of God on my side.

"I think that your first time meeting with Laura and Jessica should be supervised. I'm not saying that the Deacon will have to go with you, but Jacob and I should be there." He was nodding his head, but I could still see that he was fuming over the incident that just happened. I had taught him to breathe, count to 10 and he was doing that underneath his breath.

In the next hour, one other man from the group had decided to play his part "I don't know what the hell you were thinking yesterday, but you almost hit me with your hammer. You are just a clumsy idiot. No wonder your family left you." This was going a bit too far, but it was the only way to see if he was truly making progress. "They probably thought that you were just as worthless as I do. Why don't you just go and jump into the river and end it all?" He was right up into his face and Vance wasn't backing down. "You're just a little man that likes to beat up on women. Let's see what happens when somebody that is bigger than you decides to do the same thing?" This was going to be a telling tale and both Jacob and I were now ready to intervene if need be.

Lukas didn't say anything. He was staring straight ahead like he was looking past Vance. He then walked away, not looking back or even showing any sign that he was going to get into it.

"Where the hell do you think you're going?" Vance tried to push his buttons. Thankfully Lucas wasn't taking the bait. I felt this exhilaration. It was short lived when I began shake for no good reason. People started to yell that it was some kind of tremor and that we should find some kind of shelter. Jacob and I stood together over by the tents. It started and it had ended just as quickly. There were cracks in the earth. It really did make you feel like you were just a spec of dust in the great scheme of things.

There were several more, but in lesser degrees. It was still as terrifying as ever. People that had been through this before were now looking to us for answers. We didn't have any. This was our first time feeling anything like this.

As it was coming to an end, both Jacob and I went to help those that were now cowering on the ground. Some of them were even crying and begging God to let them live for one more day. They were bargaining and hoping that their pleas would be heard. I got down on my knees with each individual and talked to them soothingly. I saw that fear turn into gratefulness, as they once again began to go about their daily life.

It was an hour later when we heard somebody say "We need help. One of the buildings has collapsed." I felt like my heart was going to jump out of my chest. It wasn't going to stop me from rendering aid. Jacob and I both looked at each other and knew instinctively that we were going to be needed

Chapter 6

It was quite tragic and everybody was beside themselves with worry. We hadn't heard much about where this building was located. We did know that there were people inside that they were going to need help.

"I don't want anybody to get ahead of themselves. We really don't know anything at all. I'm waiting for word about what we're dealing with. The government and the military have been called in. Engineers are already on the scene to assess the situation. All we do know is that these tremors that we have recently had was detrimental to collapsing that building. We can't be sure it's the cause, but it is said that this building was not very stable anyway. We're not even sure why anybody was in there in the first place. Apparently, it was already considered hazardous." Deacon Alba had gathered us all together to speak a few words of wisdom.

"The Deacon is right and we can't assume the worst. We're just going to have to wait and see what happens. Until we know that it's safe to go in and retrieve those people, there's no way that we can even help." I wasn't sure if I believed the words ever coming out of my mouth, but I was going to have to remain strong. "Jacob and I will be going over there shortly. Once we find out anything, we'll be in touch." We had no intention of getting involved, unless our expertise in carpentry was called upon. The least we could do was be there for those that were already waiting for word about their loved ones.

A voice in the crowd raised above the others. "I need to know what's going on. My wife and child were in that area. You people stopped me from going to them and if anything happens to them, then I am going to hold all of you personally responsible. I came here to get my family and I don't want to do that by bringing them back in a pine box." Lucas was distraught and he didn't mind making everybody feel that same thing. "I don't know if this building has anything to do with my family. What I do know is that I get this feeling like I should be there."

"I know that you're worried about your family, Lucas. When I find out something, I'll make sure that you are the first one to know. That's all that I can do for now. Trust in the lord and that everything will work out exactly as it's supposed to. We all have our roles to play. When our time is up, there is no denying the grace of God. He has walked with all of you and I think that you have felt his presence at one time or another." I looked over at Jacob, knowing full well that God had provided me the source to alleviate my grief. He had seen fit to give me another, someone that was distinctly different from my husband, but still very much in my heart.

"The Deacon is right and we should all just pray and hope for the best." I followed that up with kneeling on the ground, looking towards the others and seeing that they were hesitant to follow suit. Once I began to pray out loud, they soon joined me with their heads bowed and their thoughts now on those that were trapped.

"Bethany, what you said there was very poignant, but I'm not sure that it got through to Lucas." I followed his gaze and saw that Lucas was not closing his eyes. He was now showing signs that he wasn't going to be denied. His eyes were darting everywhere and I think that he was just waiting for the right time to slip away. We were going to have to keep an eye on him. "It looks like one of our flock wants to flee." I knew that he wasn't going to do that until he had a reason to.

We were still in the process of prayers, when a young man from a neighboring village came over to the Deacon and began to whisper into his ear. You could see on the face of Deacon Alba that what he was hearing was affecting him. There was a moment there that I thought that I saw despair.

"If I could have your attention." Everybody that was praying on the ground turned to the Deacon with hope that he was going to have some kind of good news. "I'm afraid that the news is dire and that the building is very unstable. It has already collapsed and apparently there is at least 10 people inside. I'm sorry to say that two of them are your family, Lucas. They assure me that they're doing everything to get them out. If there's a way, then the engineers will find it and they will work tirelessly to make sure that your family is safe. The rest of them that are inside are children." As the weight of those words came crashing down on everybody's shoulders, I began to see that not even prayer was going to help.

Lucas was beside himself, staring straight at the Deacon, but in reality I think his mind was somewhere else. I went over to him to comfort him in his time of need, but he wasn't having any of it. "I don't want anything from you people. I'm leaving and there isn't anything on this green earth that is going to stop me." I wasn't even going to suggest something like that, but then Jacob came over and made a proposition that was beneficial to everybody concerned.

"I think that we should all go. Maybe if we are there, we might be able to convince them to work just a little bit harder. I know some of these engineers and we've talked about religion and about their own beliefs. They will listen to me"

"I'm not going to wait any longer." Jacob and I saw that he wasn't going to be a man denied. Instead of fighting him, we were going to join him. It didn't take all that much for the three of us to get out from underneath this umbrella. I saw the Deacon watching and he was shaking his head like he couldn't believe that we were so determined on getting there that we weren't even thinking straight. He did finally give us his blessing, nodding his head and showing that he was not going to try to stop us.

Unfortunately, when we got there, the engineers were not exactly ready to ride to the rescue. They said that the building was already collapsed and if anybody tried to enter that the entire thing would come down on their heads.

Chapter 7

"I don't care who you are and there's no way that anybody is going to go in there without my direct approval." Both Jacob and Lucas looked around, but there was no real security to stand in their way. "I've seen that look before and I'm not going to tell you again."

Jacob and Lucas went to grab their tools and were on their way over to the structure, when one young man stood in their way. He was too young, inexperienced and all that he could do was out stretch his hand to try to bar them from the scene. "I want you to listen to me. We all know that this is hard on you. It's hard on a lot of us and we just need to be patient. The engineers are working around the clock. I'm hoping that they will come up with a reasonable solution. Just stand down for the time being and let them do their work."

It was a reasonable request, but his pleas were falling on deaf ears. Lucas walked right up to him, stood defiantly with his hands on the man's chest and said "I know that you are just doing your job and I can respect that. What you don't know is that my family is in there and the only way that you're going to stop me from trying to help is by putting a bullet between my eyes. If you're not going to do that, then I would suggest very nicely that you stand out of my way." His eyes were wide open and he was staring daggers at this security guard.

I don't think the security guard was well prepared for this kind of scenario. He put his hands up in mock surrender and turned to the side to allow Jacob and Lucas to continue on their way. "I am going to ask you one more time to stop what you are doing. The only way that this is going to resolve itself is by the expertise of the engineers." They weren't even listening to him and even Jacob, man that was usually more pragmatic was following right along.

I went right along with them and I stood beside them as they looked at the rubble. There were trying to decide on what was the best course of action. "Are you sure that we should be even contemplating something like this. Jacob, you can't get caught up in his grief. It will only lead you down a dark and lonely road." Jacob was not doing anything, still staring at the structure and looking at it like it was a puzzle.

"You don't have to worry about me, Bethany and I'm just looking at it from a carpenter's point of view. I see that the front door is still intact. I just need to find a way to get through the barrier of those beams. If I can do that, then I should be able to find my way into the building itself." Lucas was nodding his head in agreement, even though he had no idea what Jacob was referring to. He was just hearing that Jacob was going to go in and that was more than enough for him.

Jacob took out a saw, plugged it into a nearby receptacle from one of the two generators that were on the scene. He began to use the electric saw to slice through those beams, being careful not to do any more harm than good. Lucas was helping him, grabbing onto the pieces of wood that were breaking away and taking them back out to where we were all standing.

"I don't normally say this about anyone, but your husband is amazing. Bethany, he really does have a keen eye for detail. He sees the structure as something that he can conquer. If I were to want anybody with me during this time, it would be him." This was high praise coming from Lucas. I wasn't sure if what they were doing was right, but it was certainly building the morale. People were now cheering them on. Pieces of wood were still coming out in the hands of Lucas, while the sound of the saw was still very much prevalent to everybody's ears.

"Just be careful the both of you. Don't do anything foolish." I wanted them to stop, because I was getting a very bad feeling about all of this. I could only hope that that feeling was wrong, but deep down I knew that it wasn't. Jacob was the last guy that I would think would go off half-cocked, but then again he was now in the presence of a grief stricken man.

Lucas had no idea if Laura or Jessica was still alive. All he knew was that they were in there and they needed his help. "I hope that your friends know what they're doing." This was a redheaded man with the beard to match. "I understand the sentiment of wanting to help. It's just that I don't think that what they're doing is making any real difference." I heard people clapping and we both turned to see that the door was basically open. "I really wouldn't get your hopes up. If I were them, I would've waited until I got a better picture of what was going on inside." I'd heard through the Grapevine that there was a camera on its way. It was a snakelike object that was going to slip into the crevices and not only look for survivors, but try to hear for anybody calling out as well.

Suddenly, there was this tension in the air. I felt it as thick as anything. I glanced past the engineer; saw the billow of smoke coming from the entrance and then the doorway collapsed.

Chapter 8

My heart almost stopped, looking towards the building and knowing that my husband Jacob was right now in the thick of things. He was trapped or crushed underneath the rubble. I couldn't accept that and I ran over towards the building. Everything around me seemed to happen in slow motion. The dust from the smoke that was coming out covered me and I was blinded for a moment. I tried to shield my eyes, until finally I saw a figure emerge.

Then there were two figures and Jacob was now holding Lucas. There are both covered in dust and there seemed to be a huge gash on top of Jacob's forehead. Lucas was walking with a pronounced limp. Jacob had his hand around his shoulder to support him as they came out into the open.

"I told you that it wasn't safe, but would you listen to me. If we were back in the States, I would have both of you arrested and put in jail where you couldn't interfere. I was hoping that my security would be enough, but even he is unprepared for something like this. Tell me that you've finally given up on this quest to be the hero. Nothing good can come from that." The engineer was practically pleading with them to back away.

This time, they really didn't have any other choice. Jacob was now feeling a little dizzy from the head injury and Lucas could barely stand on his right leg.

"I don't think you're going to have to worry about them doing anything. Neither one of them are in any condition to go back in there any time soon. I would ask that you do something. I will even get down on my knees and beg you." He didn't look like he believed me, but then I fell on my knees in front of him. "God sent his son down here to sacrifice himself for the good of humanity. The least you can do is try to think outside the box. You know that there's a camera on its way."

"Young lady, I don't know what you expect me to do. I don't have the Manpower or the equipment that is necessary to get in there. There is a camera coming and when it gets here, I'll try to do something." I was doing everything to appeal to his conscience.

"I know you are just trying to do your job. There are kids in there." Hearing that was making him think of his own family. "What would you do if one of your children was trapped in there? Think of that and then tell me that what Lucas and my husband did was wrong."

My dress was dirty, but I wasn't concerned about my appearance at the moment. I wanted him to see that I was serious and my convictions were strong. This was my only chance to plead my case and I was going to take full advantage of that position.

"I would've done the same thing. If the shoe was on the other foot, I would be the first one to try to bust in there to get my family out. I would hope that somebody would stop me from doing something so foolhardy. I'm what you would call an unbiased observer. I can't think of the feelings of others. The only thing that concerns me is those lives that are hanging in the balance. He was wearing a yellow hard hat and a checkered shirt that made him look like a redneck lumberjack.

I saw that his name was Henry on his badge. "Henry, there has to be something that we can do that's not going to cause any more damage."

"All we can do is wait for the camera. I wouldn't even do that, but you're being very insistent. Once that gets here, I'll try to send it through an opening and hopefully we can get word that somebody is alive."

I had done my best and at least he was going to give it a shot. "All we can do is our best. God is watching out for those children and Laura. He has sent you here as his messenger. He wouldn't have brought you in unless you could do something to help. Henry, just listen to your heart and the rest will follow." I left him scratching his chin and looking towards the structure like he couldn't believe that there was anything that he could do.

I found Lucas and my husband Jacob both being cared for by a volunteer. She was from the Red Cross and was bandaging Jacob's head. I could see that Lucas was trying to walk, but was now cringing and falling back down on to his knees. There were tears in his eyes and he was literally crawling on his hands and knees. "I have to get back to them and they need me." I had to admit that his determination and love for his family was something to be admired. "I'm not going to allow a broken ankle to stop me. They mean everything to me and if I didn't do something, I would feel like less than a man." At the time, he was not able to put much weight on his ankle, but still he was capable of crawling on his hands and knees.

"I told you that I would tell you when the camera was here. They're setting it up right now and I've found a small opening that we're going to use. If you promise not to interfere, all of you can be there when it happens." I felt like I had gotten through it to Henry with my speech about his own family.

Jacob, Lucas and myself were right there with hard hats on. The snakelike object began to slink into the opening with a wire now forcing its way through the rubble with a camera attached. We could see the progress and could hear the clinking of debris falling from the ceiling. Thankfully, Henry was able to bypass a few huge pieces, twisting the wire in such a way that it was able to move further into the structure. The only sound was the dust settling from the debris and the dripping of water that probably came from a broken pipe.

Everybody was on pins and needles, not even a word was being spoken. We all just stood there looking at the camera and listening to the audio. "I'm sorry to say that I don't see anything. That's not unusual, but what is unusual is that I don't hear any tapping or voices. That can only mean that there are no survivors." I saw the look in Lucas's eyes and he could barely contain the tears that were about to fall freely. He was rubbing his hands together and standing on crutches.

I put my faith in the man from above and then a small voice came out of nowhere. "Can anybody hear us?" Henry raised his head and looked towards the camera. It was a fuzzy image and he began to play with the dials to make it come in clear. It was still fuzzy, but now we could see a little girl looking at the camera like it was her own personal life line. A young woman with blond hair was kneeling down and looking at it as well. It had to be Laura, because Lucas began to smile like he had just seen a sight that he wasn't expecting.

As the image became clearer, you could see that all the children were still alive and relatively intact. There were injuries and even Laura herself had her arm in a sling of a makeshift fashion. They were alive, but now the problem was how to get to them.

Chapter 9

"I called in a few favors. There is a construction crew nearby that has some equipment that we can use. It took a lot of convincing, but I was able to convey the seriousness of the situation. They should be here momentarily. I just hope that they get here in time."

Lucas was the first one to grab Henry by the shirt. "What do you mean that you hope that they get here in time?"

"I'm sorry, but there's no easy way to say this. The structure is very unsound and it has been for quite some time. The kids and your wife shouldn't have been in there in the first place. It was already condemned. These latest tremors have rocked the foundation. There's actually a pretty good chance that the entire thing will be swallowed up into a sinkhole. It was the reason why the building was condemned. I don't know what your wife was thinking."

Lucas was quick with a response "I think she was thinking that she needed a place to teach these kids. Maybe she shouldn't have, but there's no way that we can go back now."

"Lucas, I don't know why you're here, but I came here to get away from you. All of that doesn't matter anymore. I just want you to know that I do love you." This was getting to Lucas and I could see that he was trying to grasp at straws for any kind of answer.

"Just hold on, Laura and tell Jessica that daddy is coming." Everybody was working together as a well-oiled machine and even volunteers from a nearby village had come with strong minds and backs to match. "Everything is being done to get you out of there. Is there any way that you can tell us of any other way that we can get to you?"

"I've tried to get through, but every time I do, I find myself hearing creaking over top of me. I've got the kids checking every nook and cranny of this small space. Basically, I'm just giving them busy work to keep their minds off of what's going on." It was probably a good thing, because Laura probably couldn't handle somebody that was hysterical.

Lucas turned to me and said "I don't know what it is, but I feel like my heart is full. These people don't even know my family and yet they are going above and beyond to try to get them out of there. I know now what is important. Life is nothing without them. They mean more to me than I can ever say. When I get them out of there and I mean when I get them out of there, I'm going to take them back home and show them a better man." He was seeing that strangers were willing to come to the rescue. It was showing him that humanity was not lost and that he could find his way back from the darkness. "I just have to remind myself just how lucky I am every day."

"If anybody can hear me, I think that we might have an idea." We all turned and saw Laura. "I don't know how easy this is going to be, but one of these children knows something that might be useful. There's apparently a tunnel system underneath this building." This was the hope that we were looking for, but was it going to be dashed or could we really make use of this tunnel system?

Chapter 10

With this new information that was provided by the kids and Laura, we were able to find the tunnel that would lead under the school. "I never knew this was even here. I think that this just might work." Henry was now force feeding the wire down the tunnel, seeing it slowly begin to constrict a little bit tighter as the distance wore on.

The equipment that the engineers had brought in from a neighboring construction site was now in the process of widening that tunnel. They were being very careful and placing beams of steel to secure the foundation. The kid that had suggested it had finally appeared. We pulled him from the area and then went to work in getting to the rest of the children.

It wasn't long before six children began to climb through the opening that we were making. Before long, Laura and Jessica appeared as well and there was a chorus of applause when they were pulled from the hole. Lucas was right there, but Laura didn't want much to do with him.

"Bethany, my love, I think that they will be just fine. We'll stop in and see them from time to time to see how they are making out. I'll even give Lucas any help that he wants. I'm just not sure that it's going to be necessary." I put my arm around Jacob, looked towards this newfound family and saw hope alive in their eyes.

END OF THIS EPISODE...

But you will probably love the next book!

>>> Click Here if you want to read the next Episode before everyone <<<

Made in the USA
Monee, IL
29 March 2024

56068451R00115